Sleeping Among Wolves

Robert Royal Poff

I dedicate this book to my grandfather, William Poff, for constantly pushing me
to continue onward in my artistic endeavors.
To my mom, Kristy Poff, for always being in my corner. And to all my friends and
family who have morphed me into the person I am today.

Content Warning:

This novella contains acts of violence, gore, cannibalism, cruelty, death, and suicide.
Some scenes may be triggering. Proceed with caution.

Chapter One

Atlas looked into the man's eyes and thought about killing him. He contemplated it. Feeling his teeth tear into his partner's still pulsating flesh in orgasmic waves of nauseating sputters. Blood shooting into the back of his throat, quenching that endless fire that burned within. Atlas looked into his eyes and could only imagine scraping them from the skull, feeling his mouth flood with intraocular fluid. Atlas looked at the man's throat and thought about tearing into it, popping each individual blood vessel with his tongue, and had to gather his composure when his mouth salivated.

His stomach starved, literally starved, his breathing hollow as his lungs seemed to push against prodding ribs, distending to layers of fat that used to block them washed away. Had he ever been this hungry before? Atlas looked at his partner like he was prey, with eyes constantly darting to vital points on some blind animalistic impulse and the vision never left, even when his heart struck so violently against his chest with fear.

"Hey stupid, is there anybody in there?" Moose called, breaking Atlas from his trance, and he realized he had been talking the entire time Atlas was absently staring. He watched his lips curl around words, but the beating of Atlas' heart muffled the sound, somehow amplified a million times over like it was being projected from an amphitheater. His face must've showcased his confusion because the man's obtuse caterpillar eyebrows furrowed. "Atlas, are you okay?"

"Yeah- I- I'm sorry, I'm listening just... zoning, I guess."

They were on a bridge, some thirty feet above a vacant street. A deep trench of woods hugged either side, encapsulating them in a secluded otherworldliness. The bridge had been abandoned long before the world had fallen apart, existing in a rusted patchwork of pylons, hazardous gaps and metal framework encased in vines. The train tracks that ran through it were missing their stakes every few feet, probably removed by the town's kids and taken as keepsakes. The road below held several abandoned cars, some crashed, others just left to rot.

Their legs dangled over the ledge, entwined in each other's embrace as their feet swung in unison, as close together as physics would allow. They pushed past every molecule between them. Discarded bottles and bags of weed surrounded them as they sat there, taking in the sunset's illustrious hues.

Atlas chanced a glance back at Moose. He was as beautiful as the day they had met. He flashed an innocent smile, crooked teeth off-putting at first before finding their continuity within his facial features, transforming to alluring in an instant. Atlas swallowed any excuse. His mouth finding different words, he uttered, 'I adore you."

His partner's smile waned for a second, before splitting his face once more, "Just adore? Nothing else you'd like to add to that?"

Atlas shook his head, and silence held their throats once more. A complete silence that lingered for seconds on end until Moose cleared his throat. "That's okay," he nuzzled up close, pressing his head onto Atlas's shoulder who had to fight off the urge to pull away when the scent of his hair flooded Atlas's nostrils, calming and homey, yet bringing with it that serial killer urge to turn and bash his skull in, to lick the juices from his corpse until it was dried. He didn't voice these thoughts, nor did he voice his fears for having them, just listened to his partner as Moose hummed a little tune to fill the air.

He was so caught up in his own worry he barely noticed as Moose began whispering something in his ear, "You know I look at you and suddenly every song has a face... and every face has a song. Like I'm seeing the world through this new lens and now everything isn't so bland. There's color in my world because of you. Real, dynamic, vibrant color." Their eyes met once more. Atlas craned his neck to look at him. "Don't laugh! I swear to God if you laugh-"

"I'm not laughing," he smiled, now almost on the verge of total collapse, "seriously, Moose, it's sweet."

"I mean it. Sometimes when I'm with you... it's like I can make it, ya' know. Through everything... despite everything. Like it's almost as though the world didn't fall apart when I'm in your arms. That all that matters is what's before us, right in the moment, not what happened or what's about to come. Just now. Just us."

"Moose?"

"I love you," he spat the words like he was afraid of them, "just know I love you; you don't have to say it back, I just need you to know I do..."

Atlas's one hand fiddled with the bong beside them. One of the few things they had carried in their backpacks to get here. Guilt flooded through him. His eye watched the slight muscle spasm in Moose's neck, his body tensing as if prepared to lunge of its own volition. "You know I'm not gonna make it through this-" Atlas began, before sliding off into silence.

The grip tightened on his leg, like Moose was scared Atlas would float away if he didn't hold on tight. "You don't know that," Moose pleaded. "We don't know that. We don't know anything about anything when it comes to this... this... thing."

"We know enough to know in a few days' time I won't be safe to be around, not for you, not for myself. That's all I really need to know."

"But-"

"I can feel it. I'm not eating anymore, I can't eat. Not any of the supplies we have with us. It's consuming me, it's turning me into one of them. A feeder. At best, I'll go mad and eat myself... at worst, I'll hurt you... and I could never do that. Not now, not ever. What they're doing, that's not living."

"And what we're doing is? Constantly on the run, constantly foraging. It's only living because I have you-"

A sound in the forest drew their attention. Atlas instinctively reached for the knife on his belt, ready to use, when a deer frolicked out of the woods. Its snow-capped tail raised high into the air, bouncing between the flora, intersecting tree trunks and bushes as it pushed a path down into the street below. They watched, smiling, and nuzzling closer as it bounced between stacks of cars, reclaiming the road as its territory.

It was beautiful, observing nature recapture her land. Atlas saw the doe prance on the hood of a red Mercedes that had smashed into the guardrail, an odd juxtaposition between nature and machine. The fawn's eyes darted around carefully.

And then it was shot, quickly as it had appeared, rocketed off its feet when the arrow pierced its side. The deer screamed. God, did it scream, in a way Atlas had never heard before. Its legs spasmed in a desperate attempt to regain footing. A man hurtled over one of the cars, making leaps and bounds of the space between them. He had the legs of an experienced runner, feet pressing the pavement in rapid turnovers that curled easily into the next step, slapping his heel into the ground before launching forward. He cleared the distance while the deer still struggled to stand. Diving like he was a baseball player pelting for home base, he slid over the top of the poor creature.

His teeth began eating before he had even come to a stop, tearing into flesh and muscle, and ripping out chunks. The deer squirmed for freedom, not dying yet but not living either. It screamed, the man screamed back, chunks of bloodied bile falling from his mouth as he immediately swiveled into the next bite. He was kneeling over the doe, careful to avoid flailing limbs as he ate, more a wolf than human.

His hands dug into the hole his teeth had made, ripping loose some organs Atlas couldn't identify, their viscous, stringy frame was a wet snake as they were pulled from the animal, still pulsating like they weren't aware they had been detached from the body. The man greedily slurped up the organs with a grotesque gulp that they could hear from the bridge, each slurping swallow permeating through their senses and raising the hairs all over Atlas' body, goosebumps formed, more out of his blind desperation to join in than his repulsion.

He slowly reached for the bong and, in a painstaking flurry of movement, shoved it within his backpack as Moose did the same with the half-filled bottle of vodka that sat beside him. Moose gradually stood, motioning for Atlas to do the same, then his foot accidentally kicked an empty bottle, dropping it over the edge of the bridge with an inauspicious shatter.

The man's head snapped towards the sound, his face coated in a mask of blood, chunks speckling his lips and his hands grasped further into the deer absentmindedly. The last thing Atlas noticed was the doe give a final kick. His hand latched onto Moose's backpack, pulling him along as they both made a break for the tree line.

Running. All he could do was run, his beaten frame barely breathing as his feet paraded an off-kilter symphony of steps. Atlas stepped. Endlessly stepped. Aimlessly stepped. His legs ached beyond description and each foot curled after the other. Such a Promethean anguish that he never even so much as imagined being possible. The pain bore hot plates down his legs. Yet even now, he stepped. Each rapid turnover pounding the dirt in an exhausted paddle foot stance. Since when did he tire so easily? Was the hunger holding him back that much?

They ran until they reached the road where an ancient pickup truck sat waiting for their return. Its rustic blue coat was splotched by a sickly orange spackle like the truck had broken out in a disease and the truck bed was filled with a hodgepodge of whatever they had packed when fleeing the compound.

They hopped in, revving the engine while their eyes probed various spots in the woods in anticipation of their pursuer. He came barreling through a second afterward, blood still dripping off his elongated chin, it mixed with saliva and his mouth foamed. The car failed to start, sputtering to life before drowning again in silence. Moose pressed the keys over and over. Nothing.

The man was gaining on them, some thirty yards out. He ran with the wild energy of an Olympic sprinter. The key turned again, still nothing. Twenty-five yards. Moose was getting desperate, cursing under his breath. "Come on, you piece of shit, work, work, work." Twenty yards. Atlas could see the milky whites of the man's eyes, overlaid with caustic piercing veins that ran fractals, cutting the whites into choppy segments. The man's eyes reflected a shadow of humanity, the desperate, the lustful, the insatiable side. Fifteen yards.

The car started rearing to life in a wave of sputtering coughs, and Moose turned to look behind him. Ten yards. Atlas could see the chunks of flesh between the man's teeth, see the spit well up within the man's throat as the car reversed. Moose drove backwards, then spun the wheel with as much gusto as he could, pounding his foot on the gas and they watched through the side window when the man reached the spot they had just been, pivoting around to follow despite the truck's increasing momentum. The man followed for a while, racing along behind until he slowed, his body reaching its limit as they drove off.

Atlas looked over at his partner. Safe. They were safe, yet he knew true safety would never be around for as long as he was.

CHAPTER TWO

"ATLAS." A VOICE WHISPERED, prodding at the peripherals of his consciousness. "Atlas. Come on Atlas, wake up."

Atlas rolled over rapidly blinking the sleep from his washed-out eyes and sat up. A hand covered his mouth, and he panicked, looking around wildly as his eyes refused to acclimate to the dark. Moose hovered over him, shushing Atlas. His other hand twitched near his mouth, holding up a single digit. "Stay quiet, follow me."

Atlas rolled out of bed, feet carefully tapping the ground as he tiptoed after his partner, past the rows of unconscious bodies that collectively gathered within the compound's sleeping quarters. For nearly six months, they lived with these people, the citizens of the compound. Shared their meals with them, their living spaces, their every waking hour within the compound's walls. Six months since the first string of infections sent the world into a domino spiral of hell.

They passed the lines of cots, decorated in minimalistic detail, a militaristic setup that bled into every aspect of the camp from its bland, lifeless interior to its heavily fortified exterior. Moose swiped his key card, silently pushing open the door and leading them out through the winding hallways that made up the compound's catacombs. They continued on, lit only by the glow sticks Moose had gathered because the compound lacked any windows, until they reached the main door that led to the yard.

The yard was the only safe space to be outside, and the only outside area the two had seen since they had gotten to the camp. Permission to leave the grand outer walls was granted to those who made supply runs. They slipped past the wandering spotlights of various guard towers, knowing their patterns by heart at this point. They ducked and weaved between various hiding spots. Being out past curfew was an offense punishable by loss of dining privileges and multiple offenses, or pursuing any harm to the foundation as a whole would lead to complete banishment from the camp outright.

They traced a familiar path, feet treading upon tainted grass as they clambered for the edge of a small dugout that had become their special spot. The sky unleashed a flurry of rain, their feet exploding into fireworks of droplets when they kicked up puddles. The canopy provided a splendid view of the stars and protection from the harsher elements, while being far enough from base camp that nobody could hear them.

Here, Moose spun around, a maniacal grin on his face, and he tugged on something inside his aged coat. He was tall, and slender, with broad shoulders made even wider by the thick letterman's jacket he was wearing and a jagged face that caught the moonlight in an intoxicating gleam, shadows pressed into his taut jawline and scraggly, distended chin. He yanked out a bottle of vodka. The label clearly pressed back on, and it was peeling away. "Care to partake, my dearest?" He croaked, a tinge of egotism in his voice as he confidently paraded the bottle.

"Moose! Where did you get that?"

"Does it matter? All that matters is I have it, so let's have some."

"Moose, we can't steal from these people." Atlas chastised. "Not after they took us in, not after all they've done for us."

Moose's thin lips morphed into a pout. "It's a single bottle of vodka. They have like a hundred. Besides, everyone at the loading dock says we're forbidden to drink the stuff anyway, so nobody does anything with it. It's all sitting uselessly in storage."

"If we're forbidden, then we shouldn't have-"

"Oh, lighten up. Besides, I know you keep a baggy of forbidden weed under your pillow, well-" his hand reached back into his jacket, withdrawing a small baggy, "kept, anyway. Until I nabbed it."

"How-"

"You're a heavy sleeper, and besides, I have these nimble fingers." he did a little dance with all ten digits.

"Your nimble fingers are gonna get us kicked out of here," Atlas hissed.

"I seem to recall you liking my nimble fingers last I checked," he made a grand show of carefully caressing Atlas's side, and Atlas felt his body tingle in the presence of Moose's hand, giving itself over to a slight shake when the pressure intensified slightly. Moose yanked him in closer, bringing their lips together and Atlas soaked in the warmth of his lover, slowly, carefully. He tasted like leftover cigarettes and past memories, stale but wonderful. He pulled away, and Atlas immediately wished for nothing more than to return to his grasp. Moose held out the baggy in one hand and the bottle in the other, testing their weight as if his body were a scale, "what's it going to be? Pick your poison."

"Can I choose the one in the middle?"

Moose smirked, chuckling a little, "You can't handle me sober."

"Hm, is that so, big boy?" Atlas pranced up, leaning in to kiss Moose before ripping both the bottle and baggy out of his hands. "I guess I'll choose both then. What are we celebrating tonight?"

"Our seven-month anniversary," Moose craned his neck towards the sky, taking in the stars, and Atlas did the same, wondering which ones had yet to die and which were far off explosions of corruption only perceivable because of their vast distance away. Seven months. Had that really been all it had been? It felt like lifetimes, six months in a socially isolated compound, leaving time to crawl while their relationship chugged at an accelerated pace. Moose must've read the confusion because he added, "It's either today or tomorrow, or last week." He shrugged. "Dates aren't really an exact science anymore, I guess."

Atlas held up the bottle, allowing the moon's glimmer to bounce from the glossy surface. "To us?"

"To family!" Moose clinked the bottle with his fist and Atlas took a swig. Burning his chest, his throat, his lips. Everything burned in the bittersweet symphony of booze that strangled his senses momentarily. He chugged as much as he could, tearing it from his lips when he could no longer fill his throat and passing it off to Moose, who did the same.

Family. The word seemed to chop the air in great swings, as if said through false lungs. The word felt heavy, existing on his tongue purely for a sense of belonging. One of the first rules they had come up with was to never talk about what they had lost. They were out on their third date when it happened, when the world fell apart. The feeders taking the streets in swarms while infection grew. They never found either of their families, and though Atlas refused to acknowledge, it was safe to assume that both of their family units had died, and besides even if they hadn't there was basically no chance of them ever running into each other again.

The compound studied samples of the infection so that everyone inside knew how it worked. Stage one, infection. Any contact with a feeder's bodily fluid would lead to the transmission of the virus. Stage two, hunger. The patient would lose all ability to eat basic foods, immediately vomiting anything dead or processed if they tried. Stage three lust. An insatiable, an endlessly driving lust for living flesh, so much that it would drive any subject to become a mad, ravenous animal.

Stage four, complete corruption. The brain remained aware, but the body became a vehicle for consumption alone. There would be no reasoning with a stage four, their body already acting of its own accord to simply carry out a desire to eat. They kept their minds, if in some small part, retaining that bit of humanity that was cognitively aware of what they were doing, but the virus was strong and widespread. Tests at the compound had confirmed the longer someone was infected the more they'd lose control of their bodily functions, first their humanity, then eventually their ability to move at all, falling into a clump of discarded flesh when the virus took everything from its host.

Atlas shook the thoughts from his head, forcing focus on his partner. Moose had a powerful shape, a fact he knew Moose hated about himself, as his feminine nature clashed with his palpable physical masculinity. He was slender but built like a swimmer, elongated muscles defined by the crawling shadows of the night. His curly hair swayed just above his eyebrows, popping out in what had once been a pompadour cut, though lack of professional treatment was morphing it into something new. Moose had never given his birth name, and Atlas had never asked, but he knew from the way Moose's reaction would sometimes come at a delay, like he was processing that someone was speaking to him, that he hadn't donned the title for long.

Atlas stepped forward, taking the bottle, and drowning in another gulp to clear his mind. The vodka ran down his throat like a hot iron, a feeling he had forgotten how much loved. Comforting, like a tender embrace from someone made of smoke and flames.

Moose stepped backward, into the pounding rain, and spread his arms wide, tilting his head back so his collarbone popped out prominently. He shook, his entire body thrumming to some alien beat before holding out his hand for Atlas to take hold of. "Come on in, the water's fine."

They waltzed out into the rain together, practically flopping to the ground where they sprawled out on the wet pavement. Atlas could feel the hairs on his body stand, as if reaching out towards the very sky that attempted to drown them. Moose searched in his pocket, withdrawing a zip lock baggie filled with dried clumps. "Shrooms time?"

"You know me." He took his dose easily, and they waited for the world to become theirs.

An hour passed under the dreary sky when the world shifted, clouds moving in funneled waves and the raindrops felt heavier. The very sense of touch itself had been idealized. He looked down at his hands, which crawled in the same slurred wake, every miniscule movement exemplified. Euphoria. Atlas was overcome with a broad sweeping sensation that overtook his body.

He felt small. Then, overwhelmingly, exponentially, large. Like he could conquer the world in a few steps while also drowning in the puddle that coagulated around him. "Are you feeling anything yet?" He called to Moose; his voice seemed to stretch a great distance to reach him.

"Oh yeah," he turned to face Atlas, his eyes tears mixed with the rainwater. A huge smile pressed his face cartoonishly, a smile that made Atlas's throat tight.

"So, I got you the 'shrooms. How's this supposed to help you write again?" Moose asked.

"It's not. It's supposed to help me feel alive, which in turn will help me write."

He rolled on his side, splashing a bit in the puddle that surrounded him. "Besides, why not have a vice? We need some reason to be here."

"How's your story coming along, then?"

"It's not... it's infuriatingly not," Atlas said. The 'shrooms took full hold of Atlas, pushing his body into an adjacent reality that cascaded in endless semi-lifelike ripples.

"You know you should stop running from your work," Moose said, half pondering.

"It's not running, it's strategic avoidance. All the greats use it."

"I'm not joking here, man. I'd kill for that kinda purpose."

"It's not like it really matters anymore... the world we knew is gone. I'm not getting published when people are out there eating each other."

"What about when things return to normal?"

"If things return to normal." Atlas cocked his head to the side like a curious puppy. His eyes flashed wide, two glorious pools of curiosity. "So, what did you actually wanna do, you know, back then?"

Moose sighed, "Doing is- is complicated. Doing is... you need a plan for it, you know? I don't want a plan. Besides, I feel like everything I'd wanna do has already been done."

"What do you mean?"

"Like... do you ever feel like you were put here to do something that was already done? Write Moby Dick or invent the lightbulb or something. Something big, but your golden ticket was already handed out to somebody years ago?"

"I'm a writer... my life is to feel that." He paused, staring up at the rain that cascaded elegantly down onto his hickory-cloaked skin. He raised a tingling hand into the air, watching it sway with a cat-like awe as his unfocused eyes bounced around the scenery. Then he meandered over to where Moose laid, making angels in the rain.

"You know you talk about writing like you hate it. Like it's some great burden you lay up on yourself. So, why do it?" Moose paused, his face crinkling adorably, deep in thought. Miles existed behind those eyes, and Atlas wanted to chase every wandering path they bore.

Atlas took a second, compositing his thoughts before speaking, "Writing is... it's horrible and it's arduous and it's brilliant and it's exhilarating and it's every last drop of every single emotion on a full spectrum. That's writing. That's crafting. That's what you have to be prepared for." Atlas let the rain run down the carefully carved curvature of his face, into each slit that creased his eyes and warped his mouth. He licked the corners of his lips when Moose's voice stole the air.

"Then why do it?"

"What other choice do I have? I was born to try anything I could to separate myself from the common man. To move the world that one millimeter. I used to think I could..." He broke off and slowly realized he wasn't meant to save the world, his voice going hollow before trailing off completely into a terrible silence.

"But now you don't?" Moose pondered.

"But now I'm worried about living 'till the next day like the rest of us. There's not really room for art in the apocalypse."

A hand clasped around Atlas, and he had to fight the urge to pull away as his body panicked. "There's gonna be more to life than this." Atlas looked over at Moose, who was intensely staring into his face. "Things are gonna go back to normal, and you're going to publish that book," he said. "I promise you." He unfurled his hand, latching his pinky finger onto Atlas's, "We're making it through this."

Atlas went to respond when a thunderous pop lit the air. Then another, and another, each louder than the next. They both sat up with a jolt. Moose clasped his hands over his ears as the earth-shattering pops flooded their skulls. "What was that?"

"Gunfire," Atlas responded. "Moose, that's inside the walls." He gripped Moose's hand tighter. Fear crept into his voice. "We gotta get back to our bunks." They stood, shoving what they could in their bags before taking off back towards camp, ignoring the zigzagging path they had taken to get there and making a straight beeline for the main compound. Smoke consumed the stars, choking them to death and great plumes ate away the sky. The main wall had burst open. A massive eighteen-wheeler that must've driven straight through crashed into the compound's enclosure, sparking the flames that devoured the walls. The spotlights sat staring down a single spot. Uncharacteristically still, nobody was operating the cyclops' eyes.

They raced each other, Moose's taller stature helping him keep the lead. They ran through the door, flipping through their pockets for the access key. Moose swiped it, and they crashed inside. Nothing. No sound, no anything. They scrambled down the endlessly sprawling labyrinth of winding hallways and reached the hall leading up to the bunkrooms. They turned the corner to a dizzying slur of carnage, bodies thrown about, some leaning against the walls while others scattered in the hall center. Dozens of bodies, many their friends, dispersed like leaves in the wind.

Bullet holes riddled the nearest corpse, penetrating the body like Swiss cheese, marred by dozens of different sized incisions. Lengths of skin tore in great lines down his stout form, revealing the still pulsating muscles beneath as blood sputtered from the open wounds. The body was torn apart, ripped at caustic asymmetrical cuts, and Atlas immediately knew it had been bitten into. The man's face was too concave to recognize which of their neighbors it was. One arm had taken a twisted, mangled formation flattened against the wall, bones cracking against each other and splintering the skin in odd craggy angles.

As they closed in, the worst of the horror was that the chest still breathed slightly. The man appeared alive despite organs leaking out onto his lap. They passed person after person in similar conditions, chunks of flesh missing in random segments like a force of nature had torn through them. Some bodies still breathed, most didn't.

"Well, so much for a rescue party." Atlas whimpered. He began tugging on Moose's sleeve, commanding "Moose, we need to leave, now!"

"We can't leave."

"Moose, they're dead! Are we seeing the same shit here? We turn back now. We get as far away from this camp as possible, and we pray whoever did this doesn't follow."

"Atlas, you said it yourself. These people saved our lives, we owe them. Hell, we-"

That's when the screaming started. A woman's voice lit the air with blood-curdling squeals and the two gained speed, rushing towards the sound despite every part of their bodies screaming at them to turn and run. They came to their sleeping chambers, peaking around the corner. Bodies littered the ground in droves, some members of the compound, others alien to them. They searched through the cluster of discarded cicada shells. A group of feeders stood in the center of the room, one of them dragging a girl by the hair while she thrashed violently. Evelin. Atlas wished in that moment that he wouldn't be able to put a name to the face, that he could pretend he didn't intimately know the person drug kicking and screaming to the center of the cluster. She was forced onto her knees, head yanked back by the hair as a knife caught her throat, slitting it in one solid movement.

Evelin fell backwards, her body surrendered to a wave of twitching as blood flew into the air in spasms. The man dropped the knife, fell to his knees, and lapped up the blood from her neck, her hand feebly tried to push him away, its spastic movement leaving her unable to do much more than swat while he stuck his tongue into the hole, sucking until his face was coated. After a few seconds, he bit into her, tearing a chunk from her neck and it was only then that her hand fell to her side and didn't rise again, her eyes going wide before falling to a terrible blankness.

Atlas grappled for Moose's arm, practically dragging him from the room as they made a mad dash down the hall. They twisted past the ranks of dead, hitting a bend, and Atlas was immediately plowed off his feet as a man tackled him, teeth snapping wildly. They grappled each other, limbs entangled in a violent mess, and they both struggled to regain their senses. The man's face hovered inches above Atlas's, yellowed teeth devouring the air between them. He struggled to close the gap, the heat of his breath mixing with the smell of vile as he inched closer. Drool leaked in great foaming globs from the man's mouth, coating Atlas's cheek in viscous fluids.

The man's eyes were wide and stared directly into Atlas's soul, stretched out eyes that revealed an even greater fear than Atlas was feeling. The man's eyes reflected a look close to pity. He spazzed, twitching into an attack, his fists flung into Atlas's side. Pain. One crushing blow after the other rocketed through his body as he fought off whatever he could. "I'm sorry-" the man screamed, "so sorry- the hunger- can't stop the hunger." Moose flung his weight at the man, toppling them both, Atlas raised on his elbows, scooting against the wall where he sat, gasping for air.

Atlas watched while the two grappled for supremacy. Moose was stronger, his frame built for a brawl and would've been easily able to overpower the man's starving frame if they weren't so close together. A fist connected with Moose's side, knocking the wind out of him, and he let out a pathetic gasp. Moose swung his weight around, but to no avail. His opponent was faster and could more easily dish out blows from the shorter range. Atlas stared helplessly as hit after hit collided with his partner's side, badly damaging his ribs. He used the wall as support, painstakingly rising to his feet and stumbling over to where they fought, grasping for the man's hair, and yanking him backwards.

The man spun like a top and pounced on Atlas before he knew it, his head bashing against the ground. That jaw cracked above him again, snapping violently as the man struggled with animalistic desperation. Atlas's arms gave slightly. The man, maybe an inch from his nose, turned his head to the side, awaiting death. His arm dropped lower, then lower still, pain running flames down his limbs as he overextended himself. He looked at those great jaws once more, and suddenly the man's head exploded.

Blood rained great splatters into Atlas's eyes, his mouth, his nose, clogging every orifice. Chunks of flesh and skull shot out in all directions. The man's body dropped, the jagged fragments of exposed bone rubbing Atlas's cheek, and his body went into full panic mode, tossing the corpse. His head whipped to the side, blinking blood out of his eyes and saw the cyclops eye of a wandering rifle pointed directly at his head, shaking violently while the holder quivered a few yards away from them. "Francis?"

"I'm so sorry, fuck, I'm so sorry," Francis wailed. "Fuck, I didn't know what to do. I'm so sorry, Atlas."

"You saved me Francis-"

"I killed you," his voice shook worse than he did as his legs bowed like he was about to drop. Francis wasn't a runner, this was probably his first kill. "I'm so sorry, Atlas, I have to do this," he cocked the firearm, a single bullet casing flying from the chamber as the next one took position, and the barrel rotated directly towards Atlas' skull.

"Francis?"

"You're infected. The blood- the blood got all over you. I'm so sorry, I shouldn't have shot him, I just- I didn't know what to do." He closed his eyes, finger itching the trigger, and Atlas once again awaited death. Moose kicked out, sweeping Francis' legs, and the rifle went off, cratering a smoking hole several inches from Atlas's head. He rolled away, slapping the ground with his feet as he slowly rose. Moose mirrored, favoring his left side, and clutching his badly damaged ribs. He advanced on Francis, who laid stunned on the ground, but he wasn't fast enough when Francis rolled to his side, pointing the rifle directly at Moose.

A banshee's wail permeated the hall and all three figures swiveled as a feeder barreled towards them. The rifle trumpeted, rocking the man's shoulder enough to throw him to the side, but not enough to knock him off his feet while he charged, flinging a wicked blade through the air in sporadic gestures as Francis attempted to cock the rifle. The blade caught Francis in the stomach, scraping a sloppy slash through his skin, and the feeder struggled to yank the blade out, tearing at flesh in jagged slices. He plucked out the blade with a plop, driving it into Francis once more. Over and over. Atlas stood there, watching him get torn apart as the man stabbed.

For seconds on end, he stood there. Just stood there. Blood dripped from his face, slightly obscuring his vision, and flooding his throat with a metallic tang until Moose drug his body around. They ran, leaving the compound and taking off through the flaming hole in the wall. He stopped, taking one last look at the compound, at safety, at their home, before they turned and, for the first time in six months, stepped outside the comfort of the walls.

Chapter Three

"Hey asshole, wake up," Atlas slugged Moose, who was snoozing in the passenger seat, taking his eyes off the road briefly to assure Moose was waking.

"What the hell's your problem?""You know the rules. You can't fall asleep near me. What if I turn? What would you do? You need to stay alert, Moose."

"I am alert-"

"You're sleeping!"

"I'm dozing, besides what the fuck am I supposed to do if you turn while driving, anyway? You'd crash and kill us both, so why do I have to be awake? Besides, we don't even know what's going to happen. Just because Francis tried to off you doesn't mean you're gonna turn. We have no idea how this virus works-"

"We know enough to be prepared, and you promised me you wouldn't sleep unless I was outside the car."

"You know I never woulda promised you jack if I knew you'd hold it over my head every twenty minutes," Moose grumbled, rolling over so he could look out the window. Atlas weaved between a cluster of cars as silence lit the air between them, cut off by the radio static which was kept at a steady flow. They kept the radio on at all times, constantly scouting for any sort of signal from a safe zone camp though they'd yet to encounter such a thing. There had to be other safe zones out there, Atlas thought to himself, knowing how desperate he was. Still, the compound couldn't be the only place that had made it that long.

"Next gas station, we see we're gonna have to stop and siphon some fuel."

"Ugh really, again? That shit makes me so sick," Moose moaned.

"I'll do it. I don't really care." Atlas looked out into the setting sun, caressing the edges of reality. It bled a deep orange into an otherwise motionless sky. "We've got maybe a half hour of daylight left anyway, then we should stop for the night."

They drove on, making odd small talk in sporadic gestures as the sun dipped from sight. Atlas stopped the truck by the side of the road, choosing an innocuous location surrounded by an array of abandoned cars where they could sleep for the night undisturbed.

"You know you don't have to go in the back. It's freezing out there," Moose pleaded. "Just stay with me, ok?"

"You know I can't do that," Atlas stated. "We have rules for a reason."

"It's like forty degrees."

"I got blankets," he reached into the back, digging out a few sheets that were tucked away. They were thinner, pitiful against the cold, but he'd have to make do. He cranked open the rickety door, slowly shutting it enough so it could latch without drawing the attention of anyone within earshot. He wavered, assuring Moose had locked the door behind him, before he made his way to the truck bed, crawling inside and cocooning himself in the blankets as protection from the elements. It was cold. Bitter cold. So frigid he had to cover every part of himself besides his mouth, but he fought off the urge to return to the warmth of the truck's interior. He knew he couldn't jeopardize Moose's safety by sleeping beside him, though he craved the comforting warmth of his partner's embrace more than any fire.

He sat there, consumed by the cold, exposed to any wandering feeders, and he pleaded for sleep to overcome him.

"Atlas, Atlas, wake up!" Moose cried out and Atlas jumped, immediately alert.

"Moose? Moose!"

"Atlas, you gotta hear this," he ushered Atlas from the bay of the truck and into the main compartment where the radio rang out. Truly rang out, with some older song he didn't recognize, though by the cadence it seemed to be from the sixties, if not earlier. Music. He had forgotten how sweet music was to the ears. Even this song he didn't recognize or overly care for pinged his ears like the most beautiful symphony he had ever heard. It had been six months since he had heard any music. The compound carried many things, including a radio, but it lacked any tapes to play, making it entirely useless. The song stopped for a second, dropping silence, before looping back to the beginning.

"Okay, it's a leftover from some station that must still be broadcasting. I don't get it-"

"Shh... listen," Moose demanded.

The song went through its dance once more, pivoting halfway to a slightly different instrumental as the guitars and drums mixed in a gorgeous duet. Once the song ended, however, it didn't begin again, instead followed by a female voice. "Attention, anyone listening. My name is Cat Voleur, broadcasting live from York College, Pennsylvania. I repeat, I am broadcasting live from York College, Pennsylvania. Coordinates, thirty-nine point ninety-four north, seventy-six point seventy three west. We have set up a safe zone within the confines of the campus. Anyone hearing this broadcast that can pass a virus screening will be welcomed with open arms. We have food. We have safety. We have a community. I repeat..." the voice continued, rattling off the message two more times before switching back to the same song.

Moose and Atlas fidgeted awkwardly, neither one wanting to speak as the song repeated its chords. Finally, Moose interjected, "What do we do now?"

"What do you mean, what do we do? We get you there. There are people, there's salvation. That's only a few days' drive from here. We could do that easily."

"What about you?"

"What about me? You heard the broadcast. They're doing scans for infection. You're not getting in there-"

"But you are." Atlas was already putting the truck in reverse, spinning around on the empty highway, and pointing them towards the direction of Pennsylvania. "Break out the map. I don't know where I'm going."

"Are we even going to discuss this?"

"What's there to discuss, Moose? This is what we were looking for. This is why we had the radio on the entire way, so we could find something like this."

"I know it's just-"

"I'm turning, Moose. Whether you like it or not, I can feel myself becoming a feeder. It's happening. This is reality." He raised his voice, echoing a yell, and wasn't sure if he was trying to convince Moose or himself.

"But-"

He slammed the brake, causing them to launch forward, caught by their seatbelts. "I am going to kill you, Moose! This is how you live! This is how one of us continues on..."

Moose looked like he was going to argue, his body going stiff before falling back into silence. He looked wistfully out the window. Atlas wanted to comfort him but had no idea what to say to aid their situation. Was there even anything that could be said? He drove off in silence, listening to the radio, and it provided the only sound to fill the truck's walls.

Chapter Four

Atlas pulled the car into an empty dirt lot, ripping the key from its slot, and tapped on Moose, who had been sleeping the past few hours. "Moose, oi, Moose!"

"I know, I know, no sleeping with you in the truck." Moose groaned, stretching. "I was resting my eyes is all."

"It's not that, we're here."

"Pennsylvania? How?"

"No, somewhere else. I figured we could make a pit stop."

Moose eyed him skeptically. They hadn't talked much since Atlas yelled at him and Atlas could feel the palpable anger that he was holding back. "What kinda pit stop?"

"You'll have to follow me and see," Atlas responded slyly, and he flashed a forced smile. They stepped out of the car, and he ushered Moose through the deep forest, following an unkempt trail that led to the sound of rushing water, a place he had been once when he was a kid. They came to a clearing where a pool of crystal clear water sat, funneled by a waterfall that stretched some fifty feet into mock infinity, catching the beams of a hungry sun that peaked above its base.

The calming sound of the falls brought with them a peaceful bliss Atlas hadn't felt in days as he took in the soothing scent of the water. Moose walked a few steps forward, gazing around before turning ecstatically back towards Atlas, a wicked grin splitting his face and his eyes were lost somewhere in his cheeks.

"I've never seen a waterfall before!" He squealed innocently.

"I know, you've told me."

"It's incredible," he gasped, holding his hands up, so they made a square and peering through it like a film director lining up a shot, "I wish I had my camera on me, I could've snapped some crazy pics of this."

"I figured you'd like this." He nodded towards the water. "Well, go on in, take a swim."

Moose excitedly reached down, pulling his shirt up over his head and whipping it off, his hair dancing as it bounced back into place. Atlas's stomach fluttered as he stared down his boyfriend's chiseled frame, his abs permanently pressed into his tanned stomach. He fought a losing battle against his own blushing face as Moose undid his belt, dropping his pants around his ankles and kicking them aside. He ran towards the water with a profound excitement.

He paddled a few feet out into the water, practically galloping as he went before stopping and turning back towards Atlas. "You're not getting in?"

"Are you joking? It's cold as shit. You're the one that did the polar plunge, not me." He casually glanced at the pool of water, practically feeling its freezing touch upon his skin from there. It was a warm day, comparatively, just warm enough for him to not question Moose's sanity too much.

Moose lingered for a second, so he added, "I'm gonna get some writing done is all." He pulled out his tablet, cluttered with miscellaneous multi-colored papers shoved into an order only his eyes could perceive, and flipped to the next available page. He hovered the pen over the paper for a few seconds, contemplating where to go next until his hand moved, one word at a time, one thought at a time, until a full sentence had been formed. He had always been a writer, from the time he was young crafting stories came naturally to him but when the apocalypse happened, he lost all his manuscripts, starting over again within the compound walls, primarily to avoid the soul-crushing nature of their situation.

Every once in a while he'd look up at Moose, who was playing within the water, swimming back and forth and eyeing up shots like he was about to snap them with a camera. Art had been the start of their relationship. When he saw Moose on a dating app for the first time, posing with his camera in every photo, he had fallen for his allure on the spot. For the first month of being at the compound, Moose had seemed lost without it, wandering aimlessly throughout most of the day until he found his place working for the packers that sorted and stored whatever the runners could fetch for that day.

Atlas zoned into his work, writing page after page. The words flowed from him almost as naturally as they used to. Dropping the page after a while, his sixth sense picked up the sensation of being watched. Moose stared at him longingly from the water, absentmindedly paddling with his feet and his head cocked to the side, slightly like a puppy.

"What?"

"You really are something to watch." He muttered, barely loud enough for Atlas to hear. "It's incredible to see your mind work. You're really into something special there, aren't you?"

"My magnum opus," Atlas said, half joking, though he didn't add that this would be his last piece of work, the first and last thing he'd ever finish.

Moose stepped out of the water, walking up to Atlas, who stood to meet him. He took a shallow breath, pulling Moose in close, their lips brushing against each other, their heated breath interlocking the air between them. Their lips swiveled against each other, hands racing up Atlas' ribs, a race neither of them would win, as they leaned in closer and closer, their lips pressing together. Sweet. Moose always tasted sweet like strawberries, with a hint of cigarettes from the last time he smoked.

Atlas took in the smell of his partner, the scent of lavender masked by a scent like raw meat and was disgusted by how hungry it made him. Their lips collided in passion fueled exuberance and all Atlas could think about was how strongly his teeth yearned to latch hold, to rip his flesh from his face. Drunken with lust at the thought, Atlas dug his hand into Moose's shoulder, secretly hoping to see blood as his fingernails clenched. Moose seemed too lit to notice, and Atlas felt Moose's body tense, turning slightly to the side.

Moose always kissed with passion first. His lips pressed softly and carefully, placed at just the perfect angle to bounce into the next. His breath was fiery, peppering steam into Atlas' throat and Atlas didn't know what he lusted for more: to continue the barrage of kissing or to rip the air from Moose's lungs. They split apart, gazing into each other's eyes as their foreheads locked. They both heaved for any air they could before an invisible force pulled them back in, like all of their atoms had been magnetized specifically for their attraction to each other.

Atlas' eyes fluttered open as the sound of crackling branches drew his left ear, tensing his body, and Moose did the same. They both looked over. There was a man standing, imprinted before the forest line. He stood motionless, waves of rolls rippling his body as his aged skin sat exposed to the elements. He wore a small, yellow bathing suit that wrapped his sagging thighs and rested under a protruding stomach, and a towel slung around his shoulders.

Atlas broke away from Moose, taking a step towards the man who didn't so much as flinch. His eyes seemed to be focused on both of them at once. He had a browned tan running along his neck and arms that faded into a much paler stomach. How long had he been standing there?

"Hey man," Atlas called out awkwardly, unsure what to say. What if he was a feeder? Nothing. No response whatsoever.

"Hey, can you hear me?"

"I ain't mean any harm," the man spoke with a slow, Southern drawl. He stepped forward, Atlas stepped back in response. "Ya'see, I was only comin' down here for a... a dip in the pond. Didn't expect to see me any company."

Moose stepped in front of Atlas, straightening his back to make his frame seem larger, like some kind of lizard in an obvious intimidation tactic. "You a feeder?" He growled.

"Feeda'?" the man replied innocently. His back stood completely straight, his arms at his side in an awkwardly still fashion, like he was replicating something human. "Ain't never heard that term before, lest you mean those folks runnin' their way 'round, gobbling' folks up." He flicked his tongue against a toothless mouth. "No, siree, I ain't one of those."

"Then what are you?"

"Cletus... I assume's a good answer to that. Just Cletus. Nothing else, nothing like... what's out there."

Moose didn't relent, his body straining to overpower the space between them. "Well, we'll be leaving then. We'll let you get back to your swim."

"Oh, I ain't need to swim, not when there's guests around. Besides, neither of y'all look like you've eaten a full meal in a while. It'd be rude of me not to invite ya ova' when I'd just about finished making mine. Besides, I got plenty 'a supplies," He turned around, heading for the tree line, but waited a few seconds, beckoning them over, "I ain't gonna hurt ya. I ain't, okay? Now, come along, boys."

Moose and Atlas exchanged glances; Atlas knew Moose was nearly starving. Their food had run out, and unless they could scavenge some more, it wouldn't be long before they both weren't eating. He took a step forward, then another, guided by his body as his brain turned off and he followed the man to the tree line.

"What are you doing?" Moose hissed.

"We need to eat, besides there's two of us and one of him. What's some old man gonna be able to do to us?"

"Plenty, an old man can do, plenty. What if he has a gun?"

"He's practically naked. Where the fuck is he gonna have a gun? Up his ass?"

"Back at his fucking house, dumbass."

"Ya know, it isn't very polite ta keep an ol' man waiting," the man called out from the woods, his voice radiating the same monotone energy even as it grew in volume.

"We don't have any other choice, Moose."

They followed the man some ways to an old ramshackle house that grew up out of stilts by the riverbed, the screen door ajar and a multitude of bug zappers hung from the porch, littering the floor with various carcasses. A fly circled its fate, humming ever closer, unaware that the beckoning light would be its downfall as it was absorbed within the canister, its body dropping to the ground a second later to join the others.

Dozens of rusted cars blotched the woodland scenery, slowly being devoured by vines as nature reclaimed them. The man walked into the house while Atlas stared at one, an old Chevy Bel Air, possibly a '57 from the build. His grandfather's favorite car, or rather, what used to be his favorite car.

"Y'all can come right on in," the man said, stepping into the house and placing his towel on a nearby chair. Atlas knew this would be his last chance to run, but he tentatively stepped inside. Moose followed, even more hesitant in his steps, as if he'd turn and flee at a moment's notice. He did, in the end, have more to live for, Atlas thought to himself. The kitchen was grease-coated, the entire house was choking on years of cigarette smoke that matted the walls and caked the air with an intoxicating buzz. Gnats danced through the air in droves, driving spots into their vision. On the grimy gleam of the table sat a bowl of fresh fruit and a single can of beans. Cletus patted a chair delicately, "Well, feel free to make yerself right at home. Don't get many visitors 'round these parts, 'fore an' after those, whatchu called 'em, feeda's showed up.

Moose pulled out the nearest seat, but Cletus shooed him off immediately. "Not... not that one. That's the wife's seat, ya see. Wouldn't wanna upset her, no way Jose. Any other'll do though, I reckon." They sat as Cletus ducked into the other room, humming a little tune Atlas didn't recognize.

As soon as he was out of earshot, Atlas was kicked in the shin and Moose whispered, "What the fuck are we doing here?"

"We needed-"

"Food, yeah, so we should've scavenged it. I mean, what the fuck, Atlas, creep of a geezer like that would've hate-crimed two gay assholes like us before the world went to hell. How do we know he's not a feeder?"

"He told us-"

Moose's face twisted in disgust, "Yeah, let's trust everything everyone tells us, why not? What could possibly go wrong?"

"Shhh, he'll hear you... besides when's the last time you've heard of a feeder reasoning with someone? If he wanted to, he would've attacked us already. Besides, where are we finding food here? We're still within range of the compound. They probably picked this area clean months ago."

"Probably," Moose huffed, far too loud for comfort. "Goddamn, if this bastard eats us, I'm beating the shit outta you," he whispered across the table.

The humming grew closer and seconds later the man re-entered the room, now wearing an apron over his sagging frame as he shuffled with great delicacy, his arms carrying a few cans of various foods. He flashed them a toothless grin, smacking his tongue over his lips, "A feast." He stated. "Seems right to buss out top shelf for the only guests we've gotten for moons."

He smoothed out the soot coated tablecloth, launching thin wisps of dirt into the air. He robotically sat down each can, all of which had already been opened, and plopped down in one of the two seats still available. "Not sure if yew boys say grace, ain't gon' force it 'on ya, but would appreciate the consideration."

"Aren't we gonna wait for your wife?" Moose asked skeptically.

The man's eyes snapped to Moose, filled with the first real emotion they had expressed as he gulped, his jaw going square. "She'll catch up, don't yew worry, she isn't... isn't feeling very well as of late." He passed a can of peas that Moose rejected. Cletus shrugged, helping himself to a pile on his plate. "Ain't gon' eat, ain't gon' eat. Food's safe, boys. I ain't pullin' nuthin."

He bowed his head, beginning his prayer as Moose awkwardly stared at Atlas, fear instilled deep within his eyes, not dropping his gaze until the man uttered, "Amen." The man began digging in first, plowing his mashed potatoes into his peas and scarfing down bites, and Moose reluctantly followed, driven by his own starvation.

Atlas stared at his plate of food, feeling the hunger within his stomach grow with intensity. A type of hunger he knew none of this food would soothe. He knew he couldn't eat, that he'd vomit it up immediately and expose his infection, but not eating seemed just as odd. His fork hovered above the rations, contemplating what to do when he noticed Cletus was staring directly at him, slowly chewing a bite like a cow would chew its cud. "Not as hungry as yer friend, it would seem," he said.

"Guess not, I don't mean to be rude, I'm just-"

"Nonsense. Nothin' rude 'bout it, like I said, ain't gon' eat, ain't gon' eat. I ain't yer dad an' I certainly ain't yer God."

Moose's eyes glanced once more at the empty chair, "So, how'd you guys make it this long alone? I presume you are alone, right?"

Cletus shrugged again. "Nobody 'round these parts. First visitors we've seen in months would be the two I'm lookin' at now. Easy to hide when not a soul wants yew found. So, what're the two of yew doin' out here, anyway?"

"We're looking for a safe zone in Pennsylvania..." Atlas spoke before he thought, and Moose kicked him under the table again. "Have you heard of it?"

"Ain't heard nuthin of the sort, to be frank. Need a place to buckle down for the night? I could always offer up the guest bedroom."

"Why are you helping us?" Moose asked, a bit too aggressively. "What do you have to gain?"

The man's eyes looked somber as he stayed silent for a length of time. "Not everybody in this world wants somethin' from yew, kid. Some people are out here lookin' to pay our dues, get by, an' put some kindness back into the world." His body froze into a smile, lingering for far too long that it made Atlas' skin crawl.

They ate in silence, Atlas leaving his food on his plate as he simply stared at it, defeated, his stomach imploding with a wild lust. When their plates had been cleaned, Cletus began making small talk, reciprocated mostly by Atlas. Eventually, Cletus called it a night, showing them to the guest bedroom, which was as disastrous as the rest of the house. Still, it was a bed. For the first time in forever, they had a bed. Atlas broke his own rule and crawled in beside Moose. The bed was warm and dry, but most of all, it was occupied. Moose spooned up against him, his muscular arms wrapping Atlas's frame as Atlas leaned back into his partner's grasp.

Home. This was his home, caught here, trapped in a place where his mind could only focus on the warmth his partner gave off. He fell asleep in his partner's arms, waking up in the middle of the night when the intense feeling of emptiness pulverized his consciousness.

He deliberately moved Moose's arm, squeezing out as to not wake him, and made his venture into the hallway looking for a bathroom. He found one, three rooms down, pissing and gazing into the mirror. His eyes were bloodshot, heavy bags swirling around them like a Junji Ito drawing of an endless barrage of spirals as they oddly juxtaposed his dark skin. His large, round nose was the only circular part of his face. His jaw had never been so pronounced; cheekbones raised in the absence of the fat that usually covered them. Skeletal. A sickly visage of his former self. He went to look closer when a crash pressed from the other room, drawing his ears. Then a shuffling, like something being drug across the floor.

Atlas rushed from the room, dragging his body through the darkness as he jumped back to where Moose still slept, safely within the confines of the bed. His body loosened, only for a second, before he was thrust against the wall, the old man holding a hand over Atlas's mouth, the man's face incredibly close as it filled the frame of his vision. He shushed Atlas, spitting a little. "I ain't gon' hurt ya. Just need to show ya something."

He removed his hand and Atlas contemplated screaming until he noticed the pistol in the old man's hand. A cold steel cylinder that gave him a deathly power. Cletus grappled for Atlas's shoulder, shoving him forward and leading him out of the house, the gun placed square at the center of his back the entire time. He led Atlas into the woods, past the line of cars and back behind the house by the water where a small graveyard sat.

A single unmarked grave sat outside the scope of the others, noted by a stick laden cross and recently dug soil that sat awkwardly around its surrounding area. "What kind of sick play is this?" Atlas spat. "Gonna make me dig my own grave or something, cause you can fuck right off if that's your plan."

"Fraid that graves already full," the man said solemnly.

"You kill someone, Cletus?"

He heard Cletus spit behind him. "Fraid so. My wife." He poked Atlas's shoulder, motioning for him to turn around, and Atlas noticed the man was crying.

Tears got trapped in the folds of his face, rolling from those eyes as the man choked through a sob. "I ain't stupid, kid. I know yer infected."

"How-"

"It's a look. Yer eyeing down that boy like he's gonna replace yer dinner. Seen that look before," he nodded to the grave, "seen it in her every time she looked me in the eye. All she coulda thought about was killin' me. Never seen eyes like that before, never in my long life." Cletus seemed to be speaking through Atlas, his voice tunneling to a different space where his mind was taking him.

"Cletus? Why tell me this now? Why tell us she was sick?"

Cletus looked at him, an aged defeat in his eyes, "Would that boy have trusted me if he knew what I'd done? Would yew have? There's not much left of the world we knew, there's just us."

Cletus hefted the gun, as though he were testing its weight, before turning it around in his hand so the grip was facing Atlas. He gestured for Atlas, who skeptically took the gun into his hand, flipping it back around and pointing it at Cletus, who smiled. "What's stopping me from shooting you right now?"

Cletus just stood there, "Unfortunately for both of us, you ain't got killer in ya, kid, not yet anyway. 'Sides there's one bullet in the chamber. I'm leaving yew with this, one gun and one bullet, one bullet's all ya need to survive, mind yew. One shot, straight through that beast inside yew, to sever it from yer bein'. I'm afraid that's all the living you've got left, son."

"You don't know me-"

"I know what yer becomin', far too well." His eyes gestured to the grave. "Seen it every step of the way. Now I'm a... I'm a firm believer in loving who yew love, mind yew. My wife Shanice was black, coloured, that's what they used to call her. If not that, then worse... almost got chased out of our own town when we got together, so believe me when I tell you ain't nothin' to do with who yew are. There ain't no saving you two. You gotta end it, if not with a bullet, then taking off in the night an' puttin' as much dirt between y'all as possible. But that boy, he'll hunt you down, mind you, I know what love'll drive a man to do. Way I see it, there's only two ways out, with him dead or with yew, an' there's only two ways yew gets taken out. Do it yerself or let the poor boy do it. Those kinda scars, havin' to live with that, wouldn't wish that on anybody."

He puffed, speaking through sobs at this point, "Had to kill Shanice. She came after me, yew see, all ravenous an' screechin'. Wasn't nuthin left of the woman she was, just... some animal... some animal is all she was. She was sleeping in my arms when she finally turned." He nodded along to nothing in particular. "He who sleeps among the wolves can only expect to be bit. Yer a wolf, a killer, simply put, yer wearing a lamb's skin so convincing you've convinced yerself yew can break the cycle. In this world, there's simply no place for a... a feeda, as yew called it. Better to take yerself out than to make someone else do it. I wish she would've. It's greedy. I'm well aware, but... maybe if she had, I wouldn't be carryin' all this."

"Why are you telling me this?"

"Cause that boy in there, he ain't like us. He ain't tainted. We're killers. Even if yew hasn't done it yet, we're bombs."

Atlas lowered the gun as it bore a new weight, one that far surpassed what his arms were capable of carrying. "So, what do we do?"

"Only thing we can do... spare the ones we love."

CHAPTER FIVE

"So, then I'm like, rushing to the stall, ya' know, and I go to open the door and someone's already in there standing with their back to me, pissing. So I panic, like usual, and go to grab the door real quick and end up just full on slapping this man on the ass. I was so embarrassed I shouted, 'I'm sorry' and ran from the bathroom entirely. It was so funny, that poor guy must've had no idea what was going on," Atlas waved his arms dramatically as he told his story, his friends gathered around him, laughing as they sipped various alcoholic drinks and others passed a blunt.

"You really are so awkward," Emma practically spat out her drink as she laughed. He looked at her hunched over frame as she sat beside him, stroking her girlfriend's thigh with one hand and cradling a half empty beer with the other. She had an elongated, pencil thin nose, with straight-cut bangs and a broad sweeping smile that half raised a pair of owl-eyed glasses. She wore a white t-shirt that hung loosely from her thin frame, and Atlas found himself unable to help himself from chancing a glance at her pronounced clavicle. He gulped, eyes bouncing around the room at its other occupants. Six of them in total. All his closest friends.

Bailey sat in the corner, practically passing out, clenching her stomach as if she was fighting off waves of nausea. Josh sat by her, blabbing on about some side tangent to anyone who wasn't listening to Atlas's story.

It was one month before the apocalypse, before the world went to hell, though Atlas didn't know what was about to come. He lingered in the moment, in his friends' jovial laughter as his face physically hurt from smiling so much. He checked his phone, almost time for him to have to leave. "I really gotta get going, guys," he proclaimed to the room.

"Are you sure you're gonna be good to drive?" Emma asked cautiously, her eyes peeling away from the movie for a single second.

"Yeah, I'm fine. I didn't even drink that much," Atlas laughed, though the shaking in his legs and the slight slur of the world said otherwise. He wasn't sure he'd pass a breathalyzer test, but he was pretty certain he could make it home anyway, the unjust confidence of booze welling up in his system. After saying his goodbyes to everyone, he stumbled out the door and into the crisp outside air.

He made his way to his pickup truck, an old beater with just as much rust as it had paint. He crawled inside, back brushing the jagged edges of a patchwork interior that needed to be re-skinned once he could afford it. He pressed his hand into his temple, attempting to focus his eyes on the road as he drove off, his car leaving behind a sputter of black smoke from its exhaust as it scraped to life.

His smile fell almost immediately upon leaving the house. His head flooded with those voices that never seemed to leave him when he was alone, bringing their uncontrollable impulses with them. The sun had long since dropped from the sky, leaving his headlights to guide the way through winding country roads that heralded barely any occupants at this time of night. His head bounced lackadaisically against the back of his seat as he sighed towards his roof.

His car began to drift, abandoning its lane as he slowly melted with the opposing lane, his body denying the fight to retrieve it. He drunkenly stared forward, daring any car to come by as he fully overtook the opposing lane, pressing his foot into the pedal until the truck began picking up speed. Sixty. He passed a sign that read forty-five but blasted past it. Seventy.

He practically begged another car to come, anything, anyone, to knock him off the road. Eighty. His car sputtered, shaking as it struggled to maintain a straight line. He saw headlights up ahead, rapidly descending upon him as he crashed forward, straight towards them.

Ninety. The car must've noticed him, laying on their horn and making Atlas jump as his back straightened from the shock. Fear overtook his body, mixed with a desperate lust as he shot forward.

One hundred. The car screeched its brakes. Far too late to stop in time, the driver obviously panicked as Atlas barreled towards him. The truck was really jittering now, wheels wobbling uncontrollably to keep up with the speed. The opposing car's headlights overtook his vision in a blinding flash, sobering his eyes in an instant as he stared down the barrel of Death, begging it onward. He closed his eyes, stomping his foot on the gas.

The screeching of the horn, the beating of the lights, the screaming of his throat, all combined into one spectacular orgasmic display but at the last possible second, he swerved, finding himself back in his own lane as the car whizzed by, still slamming their brakes. His eyes opened again, his heart racing, body parading the adrenaline that consumed all his senses. He pulled over to the side of the road, slamming his fists into the steering wheel and screaming into the void when a phone call cut through his high. He looked at the caller ID and was surprised to see the name "Moose" appear on the screen.

"H-hello?"

"Atlas?"

"Yeah?"

"Just calling to make sure we're still on for tomorrow... you okay? You sound out of breath?"

"Yeah... yeah, I'm fine, just- just out for a drive. But yeah, we're still on for tomorrow. How's six at my house sound?"

A pause, then Moose responded, his voice obviously trying to hide excitement, "Sounds great. I'll see you then."

Atlas drove the rest of the way home, unable to sleep that night. He instead took to writing, his excitement and fear fluttering feverishly throughout his chest. The next day, he got dressed in his best clothes, taking more time than he normally did to pick an outfit. He pivoted, allowing his body to carry an overly dramatic swagger in an attempt to convince himself of his own confidence as he made his way towards the ringing doorbell. He swung the door open, loudly announcing, "You're early?"

"I'm on time?"

"I said be here at six."

Moose checked his phone. "It'll be six in less than three minutes."

"So... that would make you...?"

"About to leave."

Atlas shook his hands feverishly. "Wait, wait, wait. Just a joke. So, you ready to go to the mall?"

"Yeah, I haven't been to this one in ages. Hopefully, it's still decent. Last I went in, it was a little dead."

They drove in an awkward silence, making waves of curt conversation every so often to fill the air between them as they went. It was their third date, and came with all the uncomfortableness of the courting period. When they got to the mall, conversation became looser, the environment gifting them something to talk about as they went from store to store, inspecting and commenting on various items. They found themselves in a record store where Moose divulged his love for records, a fact that Atlas found oddly endearing. Moose sashayed the stands, shuffling through racks of musical history.

"So, are you looking for anything in particular?" Atlas joined in, not quite sure what he was doing, as he pulled various albums from the rack.

"Not really."

"So, who do you like?"

"Anything really, old rock, new rock, indie, blues, some country..." he spat out a list of genres, never looking up from the records, "but I don't normally buy artists I know, I like finding new titles that have interesting covers and discovering if I like them or not organically. It's more fun that way, especially with physical media like records."

"You're really into this stuff?" Atlas asked, just to keep the conversation flowing.

"Eh, I mean it's definitely a hobby of mine, nice Weezer blue, what a classic," he smirked a little, giving off an adorable half-laugh.

"Nice..."

His smirk morphed into a full-fledged smile, corrupting his face as he snarked, "Is it nice?"

"I mean-"

"It's okay, I'm razzing you, besides- what the fuck?" A line of police cars zoomed past the grand front window, their sirens whizzing as they went by. "Where do you think they're going in such a hurry? Hey Modest Mouse, you listen to Modest Mouse? This album is a classic."

They made quite the pair, Atlas, whose mouth was so cemented shut he struggled to form a basic sentence and Moose, who was rambling, neither of them looking the other in the eyes. "Tell me about yourself," Moose asked.

"What do you wanna know?"

"Hmmm…. hobbies?"

"I'm a writer," Atlas replied with his go to whenever he was asked that question. "I enjoy hiking, video games. I don't know, pretty basic stuff."

"Write anything I'd know?"

"Not unless you've broken into my room for some light reading," he joked, watching the air spoil in an uncomfortable silence. "I haven't published anything yet, I mean. Still working my way up to it. How 'bout you? I saw your pictures with your camera."

"Ah yeah, you're lucky. I was gonna bring it with me today but my sister talked me out of it. Barely ever leave home without it, honestly. We got into a few magazines, me and my camera, nothing too prestigious, but it's always a working process with art."

"That's crazy! You'll have to show me them sometime."

Moose shot him a wicked smile. "Does that mean I'm getting a fourth date already?"

"Not with that attitude," Atlas scoffed, spying out of the corner of his eye as Moose's face contorted into a pout. "Maybe. We'll talk about that later."

"Hey, I'm gonna go cop some of these, then we can move on to the next store. Alright?"

"Someone's in a hurry. Sick of me already?"

"I'm trying to get you back to my place, don't you know?"

Moose shot him a wink, and Atlas felt his face burst into a sheen of red. He watched Moose practically skip away, swiveling his attention back to the window where an ambulance zoomed by, sirens whirring. He watched it go, zoning out into the movement until a hand suddenly slammed the glass, leaving a fully forged bloody print as the man slowly dropped to the ground, his hand sliding down the pane in a bloodied streak.

A woman from somewhere in the store screamed, and he spun around to see her race for the exit, actively pursued by another man who shambled in jerky movements, blood running down his shirt. "What the fuck?" Atlas said to himself as the woman pushed past some customers and out of the store, the man following in hot pursuit, his mouth foaming like a rabid dog. He smelled like metallic rust mixed with sweat, and he tackled the woman, taking them both to the ground and out of sight. Neither rose.

Atlas tentatively stepped towards the window to get a better look, one foot after the other, dreading what he was about to see. He was one step away when a hand wrapped around him, yanking him around. His cry pierced the air as he slugged a punch but stopped his swing as he recognized Moose's face.

"We gotta go, now!" Moose yanked on Atlas's shirt, practically dragging him to the back of the mall and away from the window where dozens of sirens lit the air.

They burst through a door that led to the backrooms, braving the alley and a collection of sounds. Broken glass. Gunshots. Shrill wails. Atlas instinctively covered his ears with his hands as Moose dragged him forward. "What's happening? Where are we going?"

"I don't know, and to your truck."

Atlas shook free of Moose's grasp. "That lady, someone's gotta help her." He made a single step backward before Moose had him pinned against the wall by his wrists.

"Atlas, we are not going back there."

Atlas struggled in vain against Moose's much stronger arms. "She's dead, Atlas. Hear me? Dead."

"How do you know that? What aren't you telling me?"

"The cashier..." Moose sighed, "the cashier, they were holding him down, Atlas. They were eating him alive."

"The fuck do you mean?"

"They were crazed, I don't know." Moose dropped his grip, but Atlas stayed firmly against the wall.

"You're telling me they're fucking zombies?"

"No, yes, no. I don't know what I'm telling you. They were talking, screaming, like they were in as much pain as he was. I don't know what happened, but I do know we need to get the fuck out of here before it happens to us. Come on, the truck's parked this way."

They continued onward, down the winding halls as Moose led the way. "I used to work here, two stores up, we're gonna get to a toy store. If we exit through there, it's a straight shot to where we parked." They crouched through the store. It was cluttered with various knickknacks, toys of all shapes and sizes that flooded the cramped isles but there were no signs of other life. They waddled the length of the store, constantly vigilant, until they reached the gigantic glass panes that marked the storefront.

They peaked over the ledge, gazing into the parking lot and found a littering of fires, sparking fireflies into the night as cars lit like Christmas trees. Nearly a dozen figures stood in the lot, thrumming to sporadic spasms as their heads whipped around wildly, almost smelling the air.

"The fuck is wrong with them?"

"They were eating people, dude! A lot is wrong with them."

Atlas looked around at the cluster of husks. "There's too many of them, and they're far too close to my truck. We'll never make it."

"You're right... we won't." Moose gulped. "But you will."

"What do you mean?"

"I distract them, you run. That's the plan, ok. You make it to the truck, then you spin around to get me."

"That's fucking ludicrous. They'll kill you."

"Got a better idea? I'm all ears." Moose's face went rigid, his bouncy features sharpening in his intensity.

"Why you, then? We should like... I don't know, draw straws or something."

"I'm faster. Varsity, track, and cross-country, the four hundred, eight hundred, and the mile. Got those kinda credentials backing you up?"

Silence. "I didn't think so," he hissed. "So let me do this."

"You barely know me-"

"And now I need to trust you. Just... come back for me, alright."

Atlas agreed, and they snuck to the door, prodding it open as quietly as possible and Moose went outside, standing once he reached the outdoors. He hollered, pummeling the window until he got all of their attention. They charged, chasing him down, and he turned to run. When all the men had begun their chase, Atlas opened the door again, heading outside. He ran, taking off for the truck, and made it to it without any complications. He dove into the front seat, pounding the key into the truck and turned it. Nothing.

He watched the men gain on Moose, who was tiring much faster than they were, peeking back at the truck constantly waiting for Atlas to come save him. Atlas flipped the key again. Nothing. Again. Then again. He was growing desperate, slamming on the dash as he cursed under his breath. Moose tripped and the first of the creatures was upon him in a second, nearly on top of him when its head exploded, body dropping to the ground.

Both Atlas and Moose looked over as a jeep pulled up. A man leaning out the passenger window with a hunting rifle took aim, firing at another one of the pursuers. The bullet ricocheted off the ground by it and they all turned, racing towards the jeep. The man made quick work of them, firing off shot after shot, most of which hit their targets as bodies dropped. The man yelled something at Moose, who quickly hopped in the jeep before they pulled up beside Atlas.

"That thing start, kid?" The man growled.

"Eventually," Atlas moaned, flipping the key over and over until the truck leisurely sputtered to life.

"Follow us. We know of a place that's safe to lie low for a bit," the guy squawked, patting the roof of the truck twice, "Yip, yip."

Chapter Six

"He just gave us all this stuff?" Moose pondered, hefting a box of canned food into the back of the pickup as they packed to leave. Atlas felt the thrumming heartbeat of the pistol under his seat. He didn't tell Moose about it, nor did he tell him about the conversation he had with Cletus the night before, crawling back into bed and pretending to have only woken up when Moose stirred. Atlas threw in the last of their new supplies, enough food to get them through the next few days, and some more blankets to shield them from the harshly intensifying weather. Late fall slowly crept up upon them.

The landscape had the early markings of winter, trees shaking off their leaves to reveal spindly limbs that creaked in an ever present wind, an absence of color plaguing them and morphed into the ground where the leaves coagulated. The days were still hot, but the nights dropped some twenty degrees, so the inconsistencies had to be accounted for. They threw on some previously scavenged old clothes. They drove on for the day, tuning into the radio every so often to make sure they were still on the right track.

The pattern was always the same, that one sixties song mixed with some variation of Cat Voleur's speech, the cadence running slower or faster, but the words were generally the same, a call for joining a community at York College. It was always her, always Cat, nobody else, which set Atlas' body in a state of constant tension. He knew he had to hold on to hope, that he had to keep up the act even if just for his own sanity. There had to be a safe spot out there somewhere, anywhere he could get Moose to before he turned.

The gun. His thoughts constantly pressed themselves back to the gun, so vividly he could practically feel the cold steel brush up against his forehead, taunting him to pull the trigger. He found himself lost in the same lust that built off his homicidal urges, and felt pity towards his own being, something he hadn't felt in a long time. He found himself running his hands anxiously along the steering wheel, plucking at its leather as he drove them across the state. They were in Virginia now, heading North as they bombarded the winding, empty roads.

"What kinda supplies are we working with?" He asked to keep his mind off the monotony of the drive.

Moose began scavenging through the back storage compartment, taking a tally on his fingers. "Like six cans of beans, five cans of veggies, and a few meats. Uhhh... like six grams of weed, a fifth of vodka, twice that much scotch, two jugs of water. Four new blankets... all the essentials, really."

They hit a bump and Moose swiveled back around. "So, the old bloke actually didn't kill us. Surprised as I am, I guess I owe you an apology, so... I'm sorry, I should've trusted you."

"It's fine... besides, you can make it up to me here soon. We're almost out of gas. The next chance we get, we should stop and siphon some."

His face contorted. "Again?"

"Again."

Both eyes flipped to the gas gauge, which sputtered. The needle practically consumed the crimson 'E.'

They drove into a city, stopping at the nearest gas station, and Moose hopped out, ready to pump some gas. He returned a second later.

"Well, do they have a generator?" Atlas asked.

"Well, they have one..."

"And?"

"Everything's bone dry, not a drop of fuel around here."

Atlas licked his lips, staring out the truck window thoughtfully. "Did you check the cars around here?"

"Yes, Atlas, I checked the cars. Whoever took the gas made sure to take every last drop of it."

"Fuck, alright. Hop in, we'll find another spot," Atlas croaked, his eyes bouncing to the dangerously low needle. Would they even have enough gas to reach another spot?

"I'm gonna check inside first," Moose proclaimed, grappling for a Maglite they had stashed in the back compartment. "Maybe they'll have some extra food."

"We have food."

"But wouldn't you kill for a chocolate bar right now?"

Kill. Atlas had to fight back his urge to kill so constantly at this point that it had basically become a new way of life. He knew he wouldn't be able to eat even if they found it, but he didn't explain that, instead he simply watched Moose cautiously case the building. Atlas traced the windowsill with his finger, scraping off some caked-on dirt as he looked around the town. Industrial buildings mixed with townhouses next to stores. A typical looking town despite the utter absence of people to fill it.

He closed his eyes and was stirred by the rev of an engine. At first, he thought he had accidentally started the truck, but no, the sound was coming from somewhere maybe a block away. Atlas ducked in his seat, barely peeking over the dash, when a car drove past. Slowly, the driver was looking around for something.

A man tore from one house, obviously a feeder from his spastic movements. He bombarded the streets, chasing the car. The car stopped, dead in its tracks as a man got out, whistling a tune and swinging a wire coated bat above his head. Atlas watched him casually stroll up to the feeder, who charged him down, not a drop of fear in the man's eyes. One hand rested casually on his crotch. The feeder jumped, the bat flung through the air and cracked the feeder's head open in an instant. The man didn't relent, slamming the bat into the feeder's skull while it laid helplessly on the ground. The sound of bones crunching flooded the air and each time the bat was pulled back up, more strings of flesh hung from the barbs.

Atlas felt bile rise in his throat as the feeder's skull got pulverized. Then another ran from the same house, thrusting herself through the doorway and skittering out towards the man. He coolly withdrew a pistol, firing off a shot at the woman's knee. Then another, both popping the feeder's kneecaps. Her face was too far away to show emotion, but her banshee wails were more than enough to reflect the pain she must've been experiencing. Alive.

Atlas was once again reminded just how alive feeders were. How they still harbored basic emotions such as pain. She dropped to her knees, and the man began his assault, swinging the bat directly into her chin and blasting her backwards. Her neck shattered instantly, head bobbing uselessly for a second before the body dropped, not rising again while the man spat what must've been a wad of chewing tobacco on her corpse.

He began his trek back to his car, lazily swinging around the blood and flesh coated bat by his side, and Atlas noticed there were at least two other people in the car. He got in and drove off, leaving the street vacant once more. For minutes Atlas was left alone, staring, on high alert for them to return, when a knock at the door made him jump out of his skin. Moose stood there, cradling a collection of candy bars in his shirt.

"What the fuck took you so long?" Atlas demanded as he opened the door, allowing Moose to spill in with the contents of his venture.

"What's your problem?"

Atlas told Moose about the encounter with the mysterious man. "The streets aren't safe, not right now," he spat. "We need to stay inside for the night. Let them put some distance between us before continuing out in the morning."

"Why not that house?" Moose pondered, pointing at the house with the corpses littering the yard. "I mean, like you said, they cleared it out. Why risk a house we don't know is safe when that one's right there?"

Atlas couldn't find any objection, so they turned the truck off, deciding to leave it where it was to avoid raising suspicion, and took what they could fit in their backpacks. They passed the corpses and Atlas found himself unable to keep himself from looking at them, their bodies laid on the grass in mangled positions, their eyes somehow still screaming with the life that had abandoned them as their bashed in skulls sputtered out onto the yard, blood still seeping out and chunks of brain scattered out around them.

He felt a sort of kinship with the corpses, knowing he would soon end up like them. He looked at Moose as he led Atlas into the house, taking his hand when they bypassed the bodies. The old man's voice echoed throughout his head, '*He who sleeps among the wolves*'. How much longer did he have before he wouldn't be able to control that fire in his gut?

They passed the doorway, dragged along by the subtle beam of light that expanded from the Maglite, Moose using it to point the way as he stood in a defensive stance, ready to strike at a moment's notice. They searched each room, holding their breath every time a door had to be opened, and Atlas only breathed again when every room had been secured. They shut the main door, closing all blinds they could find and making their imprint as small as possible and covered all their bases. They took up the second floor so that way they could barricade the staircase with a cabinet that sat in the hallway, filled with fine china and glassware.

When the area was fully secured Atlas slung his pack onto the ground with a hearty thump, using it as a backrest, whipped out his notebook and began to write once more. His pen found the familiar paper, crafting each letter with elegance and grace. Words sprouted from thoughts, sentences sprouting from those words until he was so engrossed, he barely noticed Moose leave the room. It had been four days since his contact with the infection.

Four days of running. He had three left, as most of the subjects at the compound seemed to turn completely in about a week's time. Three days to get Moose to Pennsylvania. Three days to complete his manuscript. Not nearly enough time. He wrote like his life depended on it, because in many ways, it did.

He kept at it for an hour to two before Moose came wandering back into the room. "Check out what I found," Moose hollered.

Atlas looked up, Moose was standing in the doorway, leaned askew against it, a cocky look across his face as he donned a beautiful purple skirt that barely covered his thighs and a purple and white shirt to match, both of which looked to be at least two sizes too small, his muscular body practically popping out of them. Still, his confidence was exuberant, and he flashed a hearty smile. He gave a little spin. "Well, what do you think?"

"I- wow."

"Cute, right?" He raised the skirt some, flashing his thigh and the lower part of his ass, which was cloaked by a pair of white panties. "Whole wardrobes full of shit this cute! And that's not all. Close your eyes... well, come on, close them."

Atlas heard him scurry from the room for a second and when he was commanded to open his eyes, he saw Moose was carrying what appeared to be a sizable plastic briefcase. "What is it?"

Moose smiled slyly, popping open the latches on the case and letting it drop open. Inside was one of those cheap record players that stores sold. "That's not all," Moose pranced gleefully, reaching into the void, and withdrawing a record. "'Yellow Brick Road' by the Sir Elton John himself! Do you know how much I used to rock these tracks back before the world went to hell? I mean, Saturday Nights alone is one of his all-time classics. If we turn the volume down enough, we could definitely listen to it, right?"

Atlas went to deny the attempt, fearing the attention it would bring, but couldn't reject the idea when Moose shot him some puppy dog eyes. "I don't know, maybe..."

"These walls are thick. You didn't even hear me drop something in the other room, did you? We could probably belt it and be fine, but even with the volume on low, we could have music again, Atlas, true, honest music. We won't be stuck with only our horrendous covers! There're dozens of records, too!"

When Atlas didn't relent, he excitedly sat the player on the ground, placing the record and dropping the needle. Elton's vocals lit the room and Moose began to energetically sway his hips, the skirt bouncing with the beat. He danced around the room, a spastic, uncoordinated dance that cascaded from place to place, causing Atlas to let out his first genuine laugh in a while. "What the hell are you doing?" He uttered through the laughter.

"Seducing you, duh. What, you've seen a dance this sexy before?" Moose swayed, his arms vibrating and flowing like a wave above his head as he jumped onto the couch, dropping to his knees, and sensually thrusting his hips, all the while staring directly at Atlas who had to fight off blushing. He trotted over to Atlas, motioning for him to join in.

"I'm writing-"

"You can write when the song's over. For now, you get that skinny ass up here and join me."

Atlas opened his mouth to protest, but was yanked to his feet before he could. Moose swayed, moving his arms back and forth with explosive flow. "You know this isn't so much of dancing as it is interpretive spasms," Atlas joked as his body was forced into action.

They spun around in circles, hips waggling in synchronous movements, their arms passed from one body to the other. "You know we should talk sleeping arrangements. This door locks from the inside, so you should sleep here. I'll take the other bedroom-"

"Hey shut up."

"Seriously, we-"

"Seriously, shut up, dance with me, okay? Look me in the eye and tell me I'm yours, ok. Let me have this moment."

Atlas sighed, "of course you're mine, babe, as much as I'm yours."

Moose raised his one arm and Atlas spun under it, their bodies brushing momentarily before separating back into their dance. "So when are you gonna let me read that story you've been working on?"

"Never, probably."

"Come on, at least give me a little taste."

Atlas broke off, watching as Moose shuffled around the room idiotically, and went to retrieve his notepad. He flipped to a random page, then another, flipping through a few times and when he couldn't find a page he felt comfortable sharing, he instead sighed, his mind locking on an idea he had been toiling with in his head. "Fine, but it's not edited yet, and the flow is all wonky, and-" he took a deep breath, looking at Moose's smiling face as he danced.

"In the single moment that you smile,

A thousand stars combust in a brilliant cosmic dance.

A bird surrenders itself to fate.

Spiraling groundward, its wings extended,

A moth dies, drowned in the wool of a lamb.

The Earth spins, carelessly altering the position of billions.

As it forces its way closer to the sun,

A writer crafts his masterpiece.

While his roommate hangs in the other room,

Legs still twitching above a knocked over chair.

Millions of campfires illuminate huddled families.

Gorgeous, hand stoked jewels cascade down the boundless

Curves of a model's chest,

Flaring under the clatter of cameras.

Fireworks glaze over the eyes of the blind.

Music crashes like wings over the deaf,

Everything, everywhere

Moving

Existing

Fighting for attention, all at once.

Yet still the most important thing to happen.

In that microcosm of a second..."

He paused, looking up for the first time and taking in that big stupid grin that split Moose's face as he stood transfixed on Atlas's words.

"Is your smile.

You are everything the universe strives to be."

Moose stood there, silent for a second, before uttering barely above a whisper, "You really wrote that?"

Atlas blushed, looking back towards the ground. "It's about you."

Chapter Seven

"Still no fuel?"

"Not a drop… I hate to tell you this, but we may have to ditch the truck and pick up some new wheels. One of these cars is bound to have their keys still in and some gas left over." He clambered into the passenger seat and Atlas began driving.

"No fucking way I'm ditching my truck. I bought it from my dad's friend, and we fixed it up together. Well, my dad did most of the work, but I helped where I could. This old gal's sentimental. She stays with us if we at all have the choice. Besides, it's convenient to sleep in the back."

"It barely starts. We could take our pick of these, find ourselves a nice sports car or something."

"We don't need the attention. Having a beater helps keep us below the radar when we aren't moving. And again, I need somewhere to sleep, unless you're planning on strapping me to the roof."

They were in a small, dilapidated town, the tight roads so consumed in ditched cars that Atlas had to drive at a snail's pace to avoid slamming into one of them. The winding back streets left just enough room to squeeze by with great patience and execution. "Besides- the fuck is that?"

He pointed and Moose followed his finger to a cluster of tables where corpses sat, propped up in the seats like they were having a meal, fresh food placed on the tables in front of them. Each of the corpses bloated in the heat, showcasing various stages of decay and injury. The one nearest to them had the left side of its skull bashed in, its eyes missing and the empty sockets sweltering while its hand absently gripped an empty margarita glass.

The corpse next to it donned sunglasses and a bloodstained, fluff embezzled coat like something a cartoon pimp would wear, a dusty pink cowboy hat propped haphazardly on its lulled head. The food juxtaposed the corpses with its freshness, as if it had just been placed there may be a day or two previously. A crow absently pecked at one plate while one of its brethren worked on dismantling the mouth of another corpse, plucking out a bulging purple mass from its throat before taking off into flight.

"Well, that one's gonna haunt me," Moose whispered. Atlas looked back at the road, swerving to narrowly miss a beached truck he hadn't noticed.

"We should stop at the next gas station. The sign said it's a mile this way."

"After seeing that?"

"Our only other option is running out of gas... shitttttt," he whistled the last word in a long-drawn-out display.

He slammed the brakes. Either side of the street was littered with corpses strung up in crucifixion, at least a dozen, various sizes and ages, hanging limply in the wind as their chest cavities showed through, picked clean by vultures. A family of birds was nesting within the head of one that appeared to be a young boy.

"Can we turn around now?" Moose pleaded.

"We don't have the gas," Atlas whimpered, his eyes bouncing between the figures. "Who could do something like this?"

"I'd rather not find out."

They drove on in silence, consistently jumping at any sound that Atlas had to stiffen his grip to avoid crashing. He suspiciously eyed down every alleyway. They made it to the gas station and Atlas's heart stopped. A man stood there, pumping gas into his designer car, unmoving like a cardboard cutout. It was only when they got closer that they realized he had been propped up with a series of poles, another corpse like the rest of them. Atlas flashed Moose a look, who shook his head fearfully.

Slowly, cautiously, Atlas pulled into the station, heading to an empty pump where he got out and checked the nearby cars for any available fuel. He siphoned, and to his surprise, the gas started flowing, filling the canister. He breathed a sigh of relief, flooding the tank with fuel and hopping back into the driver's seat. They both made one last glance at the prop corpse before driving off.

They drove for two more blocks before stopping at a knocked over bus that blocked the entire road. "Well, there goes that option," Moose said.

Atlas spun around, getting ready to back up, when something caught his eye. A small red dot quivered on Moose's chest. Atlas stared; the quivering intensified.

"What? What are you staring at?"

"Moose, don't move."

Moose followed Atlas's eyes, looking down and began swatting at the dot, flickering his shirt like he could knock it off. "Moose!" Atlas shoved Moose aside just as the window exploded. A slug shot straight through it and into the seat where Moose's shoulder had been. Glass coated them, thousands of craggy fractals splintering their skin and layering up on the dash. Both eyes flicked to the bus where a lone figure stood on top, hefting the smoking barrel of a rifle in one hand as he stood in a confident stance.

The man wore a gray penny coat with a white fur lining, a matching beret stacked on top of his long wavy hair and a long placid feather poked out from that like a beacon. A camera dangled from his neck; its lens extended like he had been shooting some pictures. His other hand dropped a cigarette onto the ground, stomping it out, he shouted, "Quiet on set!"

His head shook, hair quivering, his gloved hands raised, "Cut the tapes. I said cut! Pedestrians on set!" He dropped the fore stock into his free hand, squashing the stock in his armpit as he pointed the barrel at the truck once more. The red dot marked Atlas's face as his hands contemplated their speed on the wheel. "I told you Indomitus fuckers not to fuck with my set again!"

His finger itched for the trigger and Atlas's hands shot into the air submissively. "Wait! We're not who you think we are. We're just passing through here."

"Listen, assholes, I told you I'm not joining your little circle jerk! We have a schedule to stick to and films to shoot. Don't you see we're busy?"

"Whose we?" Atlas yelled back, anything to keep the man talking.

"The cast and crew?" The man's face contorted in confusion. "You must've seen the actors scattered around preparing for their parts when you were driving by."

"The corpses?" Moose whispered.

Atlas shushed him, unflinching, as he stared down the mysterious man. "I'm Atlas. This is Moose, we're passing through."

"What ever happened to you Indomitus assholes not being able to listen?"

"We aren't Indomitus… we don't know who or what that even is."

The man eyed them down skeptically before dropping his gun to his hip. "Wooo-eeee, should've said so. I almost put one in both your chests." He knelt down, dangling his legs over the side of the bus, and jumped down onto the ground, landing in a squat and picking the rifle back up. "Of course, just because you aren't with them, doesn't mean you're a sweetheart. So, how are we gonna do this?"

"We needed fuel, we've got nothing of value, and we mean you no harm. Please let us be on our way." Atlas felt his foot tentatively reach for the pistol under the seat, though he was at far too awkward a position to grab for it with any amount of speed. Reasoning would be the only option. "We're lost is all, we're unarmed."

"And we taste terrible," Moose called out.

Atlas shot him a look, and he responded, "Don't hurt to be careful."

The man shook flakes from his hair, scratching his head with the frantic nature of a dog as his eyes darted around, constantly finding new positions to land on. He didn't look infected, but he was painfully skeletal, his arms seemingly barely able to heft the rifle he carried. "Marcus, my name. It's Marcus."

A cross necklace clattered on his chest, a large silver cross that sat at a slight skew, bouncing as he craned his neck towards the sky. "Gonna get dark soon. They come out in the dark. The Indomitus. They run this area; you see. They see you on the road and you'll be dead before you know it. Best you stay with us for the night if, you know, you wanna make it through."

Atlas looked over at Moose, who gestured to the hole in the seat cushion. "He shot at me," Moose mouthed.

"Marcus… can the two of us talk for a second? Just a second. Just to talk things over."

Marcus backed off some, slinging the rifle over his shoulder, and began pacing like a soldier, talking to some invisible force as he went.

They argued back and forth for a moment, finally settling on staying the night. They turned off the truck, following Marcus to a quaint house in the district, one of the few without corpses littering its yard. "Casa del Marcus, home of the filmmaker extraordinaire," Marcus projected in a confident stance, waving his arms like a conductor and giving a slight bow. "Don't worry, it'll only be us; the actors and crew aren't allowed in my trailer. Need my personal space, get it?"

Marcus took them inside. It was quaint on the inside, every room put together with none of the usual signs of the apocalypse, as if the house itself had been untouched by time.

"So, it's only you here?" Atlas pondered aloud.

"Just us, the cast and crew, and me. Since the start, when people started eating each other. Hard to find new help after that, but we're a tight-knit community, so we make do." He sat his rifle down by a bed, smacking himself in the face, "Oh shit, where are my manners? I have booze if you're thirsty. Scotch, I think, let me go get some glasses."

It wasn't long before they were busting through drinks, and not much longer still before they wobbled back to the truck, getting the weed and their booze and adding them to the stockpile. "So, then I say- you know what I say to him?" Marcus giggled through the booze, barely able to hold a line of thought as he leaned back into his bed, "I say get the hell back into that truck and get the hell out of here before I put one between your eyes. And the man, he's quaking and crying. Mind you, this guy- he's the real deal apocalyptic asshole. He waltzed into my set expecting to kill me and my actors with all the gusto of a cartoon character and now he's near pissing himself. So, he drives off and ever since then, those fuckers have been off my back, won't even come around these parts anymore."

"How'd you do it? How'd you make it this long?"

He stared, his eyes wobbling drunkenly, "God does not call the equipped, he equips the called. I was called, if by some Holy light or by blind chance I'm unsure, but called, nonetheless. I was called here, to this very house, where I found my rifle and a stockpile of food in the basement. Old owners must've been preparing for something like this. They were dead on the couch when I showed up. So, I took it and have been using it ever since."

"And your... actors?" Moose asked.

"They come, but they never go. Some of them turned, infected people, others I found like this. We didn't know each other before but we became a family, same with the two of you, I presume. I can see it in the way you two talk to each other with your eyes. You've been close. Very close. Kind of closeness that can only be gotten through hardships together, through God's will."

Moose wobbled to his feet, "God's dead," he croaked.

"In the eyes of some, he is," Marcus said. "And in the eyes of some, he always has been. Not me though, never me. I've been guided by his light, you see. But I'm never here to judge. You don't believe and that's your prerogative."

The three of them talked and laughed throughout the night, getting drunker and higher as time went on. The sun rose, and they were still up, trying their best to fight off sleep as they sobered up. "You know, I've got an idea, you should come with us." Moose said. "To the safe zone, I mean. There's other people, there's actual, honest safety, everything we need. Come with us."

Marcus looked around thoughtfully, "No... my films are here. My art, my home, my friends. Everything I know is here, and they'd be lost without me. I'm sorry. I couldn't possibly leave."

So, it was. With heavy hearts, they bid farewell to Marcus, taking off in their truck and hitting the pavement for another day's round of driving.

Chapter Eight

Atlas's feet pelted in rapid turnovers as he followed Moose, the smell of Moose's sweat exciting Atlas as he gave chase. They swung under a tree branch, the scent of bark and pine needles filling the air. Atlas ran. As fast as his feet would allow, in any direction he could. Just ran. Every so often he'd hear feet pounding behind him, in hot pursuit as he went. How far back were they? How much longer did they have before the pursuer caught up with them?

He galloped over a knocked over tree, hurdling the branches and clipping his foot bad enough that it skewed his balance when he landed. He somersaulted into a bush, unable to stop his flailing momentum. Moose spun around, yanking Atlas up by the armpits and dragging him to his feet. "Come on, get up. They're coming!"

Atlas chanced a glance behind him. The feeder was gaining on them, rambling through the thick brush as he paraded after them, catapulting through each step with ravenous hunger. Spit flung from the man's mouth, dripping down his chin and peppering his lips as he croaked a monstrous roar. They made it to the clearing, flinging themselves towards the truck that sat some fifty yards away, shadowed by the husks of other cars around it.

Hope fluttered within Atlas's chest as they neared the truck, knowing that they'd be safe once they made it. A hope that was quickly squandered when Atlas tripped, losing his footing once more, and was tackled off his feet before he could regain them. He spun, twisting his body around and was met by the piercing eyes of Death.

Wild, inhuman eyes that caught the light in a squint as deep bags bore them into the skull. The skin on his face was entirely stretched across bones, like all the fat and muscle had deteriorated, leaving behind a translucent layer of skin, showcasing the veins beneath like bat wings. The man's yellowed, gnarled teeth snapped just above Atlas's head as he struggled his weakened frame against his assailant.

Atlas's first mistake, focusing on those teeth. The teeth of a predator. His second, not noticing the knife the man held in his hand until it swung at him, his arm barely deflected it, hovering mere millimeters above his open eye, so close it could sever an eyelash as he struggled to free himself.

Moose ran over, tugging on the man, who swung out spastically against him. Floundering back on top of Atlas's raised arms, shielding his face. Moose fought again, diving into the pile of limbs to grapple for the man's arm as he swung the knife around. Moose finally got a hold of the man, yanking him to his feet and tossing him into the dirt as he limped over to Atlas to pick him up. They ran, making it to the truck's passenger seat when the man was on them again, slamming Moose to the side where his head clanged against the truck door, an explosion of bone on metal.

Moose didn't rise as Atlas lunged within the truck, crawling for the driver's seat where he knew the pistol resided. The feeder grabbed hold of his leg, yanking him backwards as he kicked out wildly, body being pulled in two directions at once as he clawed viciously to get further inside. He wiggled and writhed, anything to avoid the man's crawling hands. They both pushed deeper into the truck and before he knew it, he was being thrown backwards, where he landed a few feet away in the dirt.

He crawled backwards, desperate to put space between them as the man advanced on him, swinging wildly. Moose stirred on the ground, drunkenly reaching around for some support to help him stand as his other hand cradled his face. Atlas faced his partner fearfully, his third mistake. The man charged and was on top of Atlas in an instant, and before Atlas could so much as scream, the knife was digging deep into his chest.

Pain, all the pain in the world, combusted in brilliant fireworks, severing his lower body as the man plucked the knife from his skin in an orgasmic sputter. The man raised the knife to his eyes, sensually licking the blood off the blade and with edacious hunger lapped the little chunks of flesh from its base.

"I'm not like the others, you know." He spat, laughing a little between licks. "I was killing far before this all started, before my infection. My family called me a monster, but, after I let them turn. After they began eating, truly eating. Who's the monster now? Maybe I'll bleed onto your boyfriend over there. I only need to consume one of you, after all."

Atlas looked back at Moose, who was still struggling to stand. The blow must've done more damage than he thought as blood poured down the side of Moose's face. "Not him," the man's knife slid under the fold of Atlas' neck, "Don't look at him, lover boy. You're mine right now. I can smell you; you know. Tainted meat. In a perfect world, I'd let you turn and kill him yourself, but I'm so hungry, I'm starving, so you'll have to do. Still got a day or two of being viable before you're nothing but a squirming sack of rot like the rest of us."

He plucked his fingers into the knife wounds, and Atlas let the world leave through his throat. The man's fingers reached around, plucking out a chunk of flesh and twirling it on his tongue. Atlas eyed some of his skin that passed the man's teeth, observed him chew, then saw him swallow. The chunk of his body went all the way down and the man's Adam's apple quivered.

"Just... leave him go," Atlas gasped. "Just... him."

"How noble of you, but where's the fun in that?" He craned Atlas's neck downward, and Atlas noticed for the first time the blood seeping through the hole in his shirt, spreading to cover his entire chest. "Watch." The man commanded. "I want you to watch as you die."

Those fingers dug deeper into Atlas's flesh, tearing the hole wider and Atlas clenched his teeth so hard he thought they might snap out of his gums as he gawked at those fingers wiggling around right under the skin, withdrawing a sizable pound of flesh, almost delicately. He felt his muscles pulsate against the air and could see them sputtering outward in between seeping piles of gushing blood.

The man craned his neck back, ready to drop the flesh into his mouth, when a rock collided with his head. Atlas studied the man while he dropped to the side and Moose took the space over him, heaving as he fought to stay conscious. A deep gash split around his eye, continuously leaking a spray of blood. Atlas, too, fought the darkness when his vision blurred, colors morphing together into new hues, and the world began to slur. He monitored the man helplessly, frozen from the pain.

Moose wobbled over, kneeling beside the man and driving the rock into his skull. Over and over he bludgeoned the man, each time bloody chunks splattering his arms and chest, he raised the rock higher. Over and over. Higher and higher. Each time the rock collided with bone, the Earth shattered with vibrations that rocketed throughout Atlas's body, making his hairs stand on end.

He watched Moose struggle to his feet, wandering over to where he was laying when Moose called out to him with words Atlas couldn't catch. He seemed far away. Far too far away, as Atlas was rapidly losing consciousness. He saw Moose's mouth move, projected by false lungs like a doll on loosely wired strings, all the while Moose wrapped those muscular arms around Atlas. Atlas burned like his entire body had been set on fire. He looked into Moose's eyes, and he thought, this is what death must feel like. Burning. He stared for as long as he could between heavy blinks, making sure Moose's gorgeous eyes would be the last thing he saw when he died in Moose's arms.

"Moose... I don't wanna go, Moose. Don't make me go," he begged, clawing for Moose's face.

Moose simply shushed him, cooing, "you're not going anywhere. You're staying right here; you're staying with me. Just hold on tight... just... just hold on tight."

Moose carried him to the passenger seat of the truck. Slipping on the pool of blood that had coagulated, he dropped Atlas inside. Blood surrounded them, drenching their clothes so badly that Atlas couldn't tell which was his and which was Moose's as it sprayed onto the car seat and floor. Atlas couldn't feel his body anymore, anything below his chest so numb it might as well had stopped existing while he fought to keep his eyes open.

Just one more, he thought to himself with every blink. One more look into Moose's eyes. That was all he needed, one more. He wanted for nothing more than to put his hand on Moose's cheek, to soothe those wild eyes meanwhile Moose's sobbing tears intermixed the dripping blood. Just let him live, Atlas thought. Maybe he'd even be better off without him.

Atlas closed his eyes, and this time, they didn't open. He still felt the world around him, heard the revving of the truck in the distance, felt Moose's hand on his chest, but his eyes refused to take in the world any longer. One by one, his senses dipped out of existence, leaving him with only darkness.

Chapter Nine

Atlas came back into existence the same way he had the first time, kicking and screaming. He bit down on something that had been wedged between his teeth. Gripped a pile of sheets in barely functional hands. His eyesight was the last sense to return to him, coming in spurts of nauseating spirals of light and bustling bodies that would momentarily hang over him before the darkness corrupted his vision once more. The people donned masks, their faces coming in waves as movement seemed to slide in and out of existence, everything and anything coming in streaks of flashing lights.

Disorientating. Everything around him as reality slurred. He screamed, calling out in false tongues he couldn't hear as the pain bore hot plates down his body. Such an excruciating anguish that he had felt nothing close to as the figures over him dropped something liquid onto his open wound, which tore his very being like shattered glass. He looked down and saw the flash of various metal instruments protruding from his chest before something forced his chin upward. A figure pulled down their mask, mouthing words that never quite made it to Atlas's ears. His eyes must've showcased panic as the woman got closer. "Eyes on me." She mouthed, slowly, moving her mouth muscles in grand gestures around each syllable.

He laid there fearfully as that face disappeared for a bit, reappearing after what could've been several seconds or minutes as the pain made time nonexistent. He fought to keep his eyes open as his eyelids weighed down his face, closing and reopening on their own will. "Just keep your eyes on me," the woman said, her voice finally reaching his ears as various shouting voices began permeating throughout the air, vaporizing any details like a noise soup.

He passed out in spurts, coming to just as suddenly, each time with a bit more permanence, and coming a bit stronger. Soon, the instruments disappeared from his body, as did the voices and wandering phantoms that crossed his vision in increasingly seldom intervals. After his fourth or fifth time coming to, he was met by a hand holding his, gripping it in a vice-like hold. His eyes moved before his head, lackadaisically swiveling on a heavy, rusted pivot. The figure holding his hand came at a jumble of details like a Picasso painting, coming into being after a few seconds of staring into the cascading light.

Moose stared back at him, a look of concern stamped his face. "Hey, Atlas, you awake?" He raised Atlas's hand to his face, planting a soft kiss on his knuckles and holding the hand up to his cheek.

"Don't you ever fucking scare me like that again, you hear me?"

Atlas stared, wanting so badly to speak, but his mouth remained cemented shut. "Don't speak, okay, relax," Moose replied, as if reading his mind. "You need to take the day to heal. We'll start back up in the morning. They tell me we're a day's drive from the college, we're almost there, Atlas. We're truly, actually gonna be there."

Atlas switched gears immediately, voicing his fears as quickly as he could in his slurred state, "Moose, the blood... his blood. Did you get any in your eyes... in your cut?"

"I... I don't know." His feet scraped the ground awkwardly, drawing some spirals.

"You have to know."

"I don't think so, ok. They don't think so. The doctors here. But we have more important things to worry about."

"Moose-"

"It'll be okay, Atlas, I'll be okay. I promise, I feel... well, not fine. I feel like I've been bludgeoned half to death, but I feel like me, regular ol' me."

Atlas stared in response. "Oh yeah, I should introduce you to everyone. They'll love to hear you're finally awake! Can you stand?" Moose replied.

He wobbled over and Atlas only now noticed the stitches running down his head, a railroad track that looped around his eye and down the bridge of his nose. His one eyelid drooped in a way it hadn't before and lines of raised bruising wrapped the stitches, making them even more apparent. He stooped down, wrapping a toned arm around Atlas and helping him to his feet. They teetered to their feet, heading out of the tent and into the blinding light of the outside. They were about thirty feet away from a line of train cars, all of which heralded various encampments, canopies protruding from them as people walked from car to car.

All women, each one of them, besides Moose and Atlas. They hobbled down the length of a few carts. Each one had a sleeping bag of various sizes sprawled out, some with multiple, as well as a collection of knickknacks, weapons, foods, and medicines. A woman slept in the one cart, while others hung clothes from lines to dry. Some waved, some slept, others stood guard, weapons in hand. A full community, bottled into the lengths of carts that ran down the tracks.

"Pretty crazy, right?" Moose spoke as they walked along. He stopped, motioning for Atlas to do the same as they rounded to another train cart, this one with the broad metal doors closed. "This is the one," Moose said, without further explanation. He rapped his knuckles on the door. An echoing twang filled the air. A few seconds of silence followed, then the whirling of a door being unlocked as the great door creaked open. Inside was a medical bay, the same room that Atlas remembered being in during his surgery, and his fingers instinctively scraped the throbbing line of railroad tracks that ran down his chest.

A woman met them inside, donning a blood splattered coat and bright blue medical gloves that looked to be multiple sizes too large, the latex sagging under its own weight. They locked eyes, and a smile split the woman's face. "I see our patients up and active!"

Atlas went to speak, but the air was stolen from him as the woman sputtered, "How do you like my handiwork? I'm no doctor, and this is certainly far from a suitable space to perform such a surgery, but I think I did a pretty bang-up job, if I do say so myself. As long as the infection stays away, I expect even the scarring won't be terrible!" She held out a hand before retracting it for a second, biting the glove off her fingers, and holding it out again. "The name's Willow, by the way."

They shook, Willow delicately moving Atlas's hand in short, fluid movements. "You're gonna have to baby it for a while. If you pull those stitches, I can't promise I'll be able to fix it to the same extent. Besides, it'll be incredibly painful so, rest up, doctor's orders."

Willow motioned for Moose to offer his arm, using it as a hoist to jump from the wagon, and brushed some dirt off her scrubs. "I'll show you around, both of you. You know, Atlas, Moose had to be forced from your side. He's barely seen most of our encampment, too."

Willow began showing them around, talking the entire time about different parts of the camp and their history over the last six months. The camp was divided into three parts. The main section, the train cars functioned as homes and storage, making up the bulk of the camp's activities. The second section was outer encampments made of tents circled around fire pits where newer occupants slept and lived. The third section was a hodgepodge of randomly scattered watchtowers, built out of a collection of various metal sheets, car doors, and wooden pylons.

Willow explained that the camp housed an impressive fifty-two occupants, some of which had been there since the beginning, others for a few days, all of which were women. The camp only allowed for women to stay to live within its safety, as it had been started by an abuse victim support group that had stumbled across the abandoned train within the first few days of the virus spreading. Willow also explained how runners had found their truck, still running by the side of the road where Moose must've passed out. The runners took them in, fixing their wounds and letting them stay within the camp to heal despite the rules regarding keeping men.

Moose remained uncharacteristically quiet throughout the tour. His eyes seemed false, like they had been replaced with marbles while Atlas was under. His face was a blank sleet, all color and character stripped away to reveal a mannequin-like replica of its former self. They went to the outskirts of the camp to where a little ledge overlooked the entire encampment. The train went for maybe thirty some cars, snaking its way down the tracks so far Atlas had to make a mental panorama to capture the visage of it all. Quiet. Despite so many people being below them, everything was steady, peaceful.

Moose swung his legs over the ledge, plopping down, and his thousand-yard stare wrapped nothing in particular. Atlas walked up to him, his hand extending a bottle of booze, tapping it onto Moose's shoulder. Moose didn't even look towards it, his hand rejecting it immediately, and Atlas sat beside him, Willow sitting down a few feet off. Atlas put his head on Moose's shoulder, nuzzling into the crevice between his shoulder and jawline. "You okay, big guy?"

Moose's eyes never dropped from that one spot, his hands spastically wiping some invisible something off them and onto his pants. "My hands, these hands."

He croaked. "I've tried to wash off the blood, but I can still feel it on there, constantly, always on there. I've scrubbed and scrubbed, and I can still see it. Blood. Everywhere. Between the cracks, under my fingernails, polluting my vision." A tear fell down his cheek, a single line of water that made a path down his pores. "I killed someone, Atlas. That man, he was attacking you and all I saw was red. No, not even red, I saw nothing. I woke up and his skull was on my hands. His life was inside me, consumed by me."

"I know…" But Atlas knew he had no idea how to help, nor what to say. What would've even equipped him for such a conversation, to condone murder in defense of his own life? "I would've died, he would've killed us-"

"I don't know if any of that matters. I killed him regardless of circumstance. Every time I think about it, I want to vomit. It's the one thing I see when I close my eyes. It's the one thing I can feel. His blood was so warm on my skin, his bones so coarse. His brain peppered my clothes. What do I do now? How do I do now?

"We move on. We find a way to move on and we keep on living."

"How? How do I move on Atlas? I killed a man, I-"

"He was going to kill me!" Atlas jumped at the intensity of his own voice. "He was going to kill us! You did nothing wrong!"

Moose opened his mouth, letting his lip quiver for a second before closing it again, staring silently. Nothing, his face still reflected nothing, even as tears streamed down. Atlas went to entangle his leg around Moose's, slowly snaking their toes together, but Willow let out a scream.

All three pairs of eyes went to the edge of the camp, where a plume of smoke choked the air. Screaming erupted from the camp and before he knew it, Willow was running off. Atlas stood to follow, taking a few steps before realizing Moose wasn't following. "Moose, we gotta go," he hissed. "Come on." He tugged on Moose's arm, who didn't budge an inch. "Moose, what's wrong?"

Moose's arm dropped limply by his side. "I can't."

"You… can't?"

"I can't do it. I'm sorry I can't. I can't kill… not again." His eyes flicked to the smoke.

Atlas knelt down beside Moose, delicately turning his head so that both eyes were looking at him. That face, that Frankensteined face, stared back at him solemnly. "Moose, Moose, Moose, look at me. Look, we gotta decide, and we gotta decide fast. Do we go down to the camp or do we drive off? I don't care whichever we do. I'm sorry, I don't care about them." Atlas sat there, waiting for Moose to combat him, to sacrifice himself like he knew he would and demand to go back to the camp to save the day, but Atlas' stomach dropped as Moose didn't relent, not even trying to convince Atlas to stay.

Atlas' heart broke as Moose dropped the next phrase, "I don't know... maybe we should leave."

"Are- are you sure? If that's what you want, we'll leave now, but make sure because once we do, there's no going back."

Moose turned towards Atlas, "I can't see those eyes. Not again."

"Then let's go." he held out his hand, waiting for Moose to take it. "I saw the truck while-" he almost slipped, saying the name of the girl he knew they were abandoning. "I saw the truck. We should be able to get to it while avoiding whatever's happening down there."

Moose gave a slight nod, his eyes never leaving the burning boxcars. What was happening down there? Atlas didn't know, nor did he want to, as the thought of abandoning the people that saved him made his stomach churn. Still, he looked into Moose's eyes, those fractured, punctured eyes that sobbed tearlessly, and knew he had to look out for Moose and Moose alone.

They crept down the hill, careful to avoid the commotion as gunfire lit the air in starved cannons. They retraced the steps that Willow had shown them, until they reached a clearing where a line of cars sat, ready for use whenever needed, and right in the middle of them was Atlas' old beater. He felt for his pocket where the keys still resided, anxiously running his thumb down its jagged base. The only weapon they had on them as they'd have to pass through the open field, a pitiful little safety net.

They crouched, duck walking past lines of cars, their eyes whipping around at every thunderous gunshot or scream. Atlas could hear voices getting closer, some yelling, some laughing. They crept out past a gap in the cars and Atlas saw a woman being forced to her knees, squirming as she fought against her oppressors. The one man brandished a machete, whipping it around wildly before pressing it under her chin.

He cackled caustically, raising her chin and reeled back a slash that never made contact with the poor woman as half his head exploded, his eye cascading from his face and into the dirt as his body soon followed. The other men returned fire, one of them apparently hitting their target as they ceased and returned to the girl who had already stumbled to her feet, breaking off into the woods. A round of bullets followed her, but Atlas couldn't see if they had reached their target or not.

They continued onward, past the ranks of grounded vehicles until a man stumbled out in front of them, gripping something in his arms that he held tight to his stomach, blood licking trails down his side from a wound his hands covered. He made the mistake of moving his hand and whatever he was holding dropped to the ground. At first it appeared like a wet snake, uncoiling as it fell in moist sputters. Organs. The man's intestines dropped from a deep gash in his body, and he stumbled a few more steps without them, his body unaware of the death it lingered in as his eyes met Atlas's right before he dropped to the ground, unmoving.

Moose and Atlas had to step over the body as they continued forward, finally making it to the lemon. They hopped inside, attempting to slowly close the door to prevent as much sound as possible. Atlas put the car in reverse, not daring to step on the gas as they drifted from the spot. They made it maybe five feet when a bullet ricocheted off the side of the truck with a metallic twang. Atlas flipped the car into drive, stomping the gas, and they were gone before their pursuers fired another shot.

Chapter Ten

ATLAS CHANCED A GLANCE into the truck window, making sure Moose was still asleep, before slinging his pack over his back. He had silently split the supplies into two piles, taking the smaller amount, as much as he could fit into the pack, and took off into the night, following the light of the stars as he went. "He who sleeps among the wolves can only expect to be bit," rang out throughout Atlas's head over and over, constantly crashing his thoughts as his blood rang out. His blood was flowing through his veins. He could feel it. The hunger was so strong it nearly brought him to tears.

He wanted to tear into Moose's skin, to envelop it, to truly enter him and live within his skin. To devour him, his flesh, his core, to rip every fiber from his being. "He who sleeps among the wolves," he was degrading into an animal. Nothing more, nothing less. Even walking away, his body threatened to turn around, to break through the window and gut Moose with the broken glass. He hobbled off, the wound on his chest burning with every inhale, soothed through the exhale as he could feel his muscles shifting around the new hole, desperately trying to function as normal.

He walked until the sun rose, putting as much distance between him and Moose as he could, his legs threatening to collapse as he galloped down the road. Every once in a while, he'd check a car for its keys. Some were still in the ignitions, but none would start. Hunger. All he could think about was his hunger. It must've been going on seven days since he had eaten last, his mind bubbling in unconscious sways. Is this how they all felt? It was more than enough to drive him mad. He stopped, cramming a few pieces of canned peaches down his throat in a desperate attempt to soothe the beating starvation, but threw it up almost immediately, emptying his stomach even more as blood mixed with the bile.

He looked at his reflection in a puddle and was surprised by how unrecognizable he had become. His dark skin had noticeably paled, his thick nose providing the only subtle curvature in a jagged face that pushed the word gaunt to an unfathomable degree, as the hairs that sprouted up got lost in the contours. His eyes were near popping from a defined skull, looking as though they might fall out at the slightest movement. Two crystalline eyes that mocked life from within an empty vessel.

He splashed water onto his face, trying to cleanse the grime that had formed a constant mask onto his skin, but as he scrubbed, he only revealed more layers. How long had it been since he had actually cleaned? He heard the sputter of an engine, his head shooting up as if on a spring and craning around towards the source of the noise. A car drove by, shooting through the street at such an insane speed that Atlas could see the tires wobble as they tried to keep up. The car drove directly into a beached truck, screeching with a thunderous impact and all the airbags deployed as the cars ping-ponged off one and into another.

He ran over to the car, his eyes locked on the driver's seat, where a figure slumped against the deployed airbag. He fought to open the crunched in door, putting all his weight into inching it open. He pushed the airbag from his way, attempting against logic to flatten it as the man inside limply sat. A fire lapped up from under the hood, peaking out in spastic tendrils, and Atlas knew he didn't have long before the entire vehicle would be in flames.

He grappled for the man's broken arm, tugging it, but the mangled bones didn't allow for much movement. He reached in further, pulling the man by the armpits as the flames rose over the dash, shooting off an intense amount of heat and pressure.

Atlas tugged the man from his seat, dropping him onto the pavement and dragging him from the car. They were maybe five yards from it when the engine combusted, launching a fireball into the air that nearly shot Atlas off his feet as the entire car exploded in flames. Atlas dropped, panting, beside the man, both of them laying on the middle of the highway. Atlas laid there for a while, reclaiming breath in his lungs as a stabbing pain consumed him.

He looked over at the man. His jaw was broken, laying limply on the ground in a stretched exuberance the typical bone structure wouldn't have allowed for. His eyes pierced, filled with life as they stared at Atlas, constantly darting around, and Atlas wasn't sure the man could scream from the pain even if he wanted to. The man's good arm raised a little, scratching at his shirt as his eyes pressed into Atlas even harder. Atlas rolled over, crawling up onto the man's chest, ignoring the popping of his shattered bones as they displaced, and unraveled the man's shirt.

A chunk had been taken out of his shoulder, the distinguishable size and shape to be a bite mark, standing out even among the wreckage of his body, and Atlas knew instantly what had happened. The man was infected. Atlas' nose twitched towards the bloody wound, lowering towards it of his body's own will. The smell of blood, of rot, was intoxicatingly sweet as he got closer. He struggled against his own body as it dropped further, drool falling from his lips and mixing in with the blood that coagulated around the open wound.

The entire time, the man's eyes stared fearfully at him, just stared, judgingly. Atlas didn't leave those eyes, letting them consume his vision as his tongue pressed into the wound, lapping up a bit of blood and drawing it into his mouth, swallowing reluctantly as it flooded his taste buds with a sickening sweetness. He stuck his tongue in deeper, feeling the muscles pulsate around his tongue, like vaginal walls closing and opening as his phallic tongue pushed even deeper, consuming whatever it could as it went.

His teeth brushed the wounds walls, closing around skin and yanking it into the back of his throat where it shot viscous fluids, every bit as sensual as his first-time having sex as the lingering sputters of muscle clashed orgasmically against his cheeks. He tore a chunk, snapping it between his teeth and swallowing load after load. The entire time, those eyes simply watched him, unable to do as much as look away as the man's crippled body became the first home Atlas had found in months.

He kissed the area around the wound, puckering as great globs filled his mouth. Each swallow calmed that rigorous flame that burst from his stomach, so strong of a desire that he found the world around him melt away, his entire being repurposed into eating and eating alone.

He wasn't sure how long it took him to eat the man, nor how far into it the man died, those eyes trapped within the same fear for eternity as they still stared, not even blinking. Atlas sat backwards, leaning against the guardrail as he stared at what was left of the corpse, sickeningly craving more, even as he was terrified by what he had done. He stood, running from the corpse and into a small river that sat beside the road, cleansing himself of the blood that coated his front. Is this what it felt like to have turned? He was surprised by how much of his sanity he reclaimed, how much he knew his actions were wrong, were disgusting, yet still he couldn't stop himself. He washed off his skin and knew the blood would never truly wash away.

After he felt he was as clean as he could get himself, he began his advance forward once more, using the road to guide him. The hunger came back quickly, maybe a day after he had devoured what he had of the corpse, as though this was all he could do from now on. Consume. Just that, consume.

When he could walk no further, he found a shady spot by a couple of trees, sitting down and withdrawing his manuscript from his bag. He wrote. Endlessly, aimlessly writing until his fingers hurt. Anything to keep him from the thought of returning to the corpse. He thought about Moose, about how much he missed him. But he knew he'd never want Moose to see him again, not like this, not after becoming what he had become. He stabbed the pen into the paper and crafted his story, word by word, brick by brick, finally ending on the last page in the notebook, where he slapped the final word to the piece, ending it in all its glory.

It was sloppy, unedited and unconventional, but he smiled as he stickered those final two words to his work, "the end." He wasn't sure what feeling he felt next. Relief. Anguish. Fear. Depression. All he knew was it was done as he let the pen roll from his hand, dropped into the void surrounding him. One hundred and twenty-two pages of written word stacked before him, an accumulation of six months of tireless work, the first and only thing he had ever truly finished. He sighed, weighed down by the knowledge that his story would never actually be read. Still, he felt an immense pride in himself and couldn't help but stare at his work like a father watching his child walk for the first time.

He slept there for the night. Then began again in the morning. He could feel his brain liquifying from the infection, thoughts becoming harder to gain tangibility, memories harder to pull from. He knew this would be one of if not the last day as himself, but he had no idea what he wanted to do with it. No, he knew what he wanted; he wanted to cry out to Moose. To feel his embrace one last time, feel the calming presence of his lover's voice. Love. He had never said the word to Moose before, but it was all he could think about now. His limbs jerked as he moved, as if separating themselves from the brain and finding their own consciousness as they pushed him forward and his nose constantly sniffed the air for fresh meat. He was losing intuitions, his sense of self-preservation dropping off his mind as he no longer snuck around but strode out into the road, confidently seeking his next meal.

Cletus' words echoed throughout his skull, on a constant loop though the phrasing muddied as the hunger constricted his brain, trapping within it any details. His tongue flicked around inside his mouth, constantly seeking its next meal as it dried from the heat. He sympathized with the infected for maybe the first time, no longer seeing them as monsters as the hunger drove him mad. Yet still he walked in what direction he wasn't sure. Eight days. It had to have been around eight days since his infection.

He trudged onward, aimlessly wandering, his mind so wrapped up in its own liquidation that he didn't even notice the truck until he was caught in its head-lights.

CHAPTER ELEVEN

MOOSE HAD FOUND HIM. He wanted to scream, to run off for the woods, but his legs wouldn't allow the movement as he just stood there. Moose stared back at him through the broken glass of the front windshield. Seconds became minutes. Cletus' words echoed throughout Atlas' skull, "but that boy, he'll hunt you down. Mind you, I know what love'll drive a man to do." How had he known? The entire time he had known. How was Moose able to track Atlas so far?

Moose drove forward a bit, so the truck lined up with Atlas. The entire time they never took their eyes off each other, as if testing the others will to escape. Moose pat the seat beside him, smiling, "You know I don't normally pick up hitchhikers-"

"Why did you follow me?" Atlas pressed, standing his ground.

Moose's smile dropped into the shadow of a frown. "I've been searching for you since you left-"

"That doesn't answer my question. You shouldn't have followed me. Why did you follow me?" He was shouting now, acutely aware of the lingering stickiness the dried blood residue left on his chest and neck.

"Just get in the car," Moose pleaded.

"Not until-"

"Just get in the fucking car!" Moose roared so vigorously that spit flew from his lips. "We don't fucking do this! We don't leave each other. Our plan was always to get there. Together!"

"No, our plan was to always get you there, Moose! You! You refused to listen to reason. Do you want to die? I'm a killer, a wolf; you're going to die at my hands, Moose! I can't let that happen. I-"

Atlas froze as Moose's body suddenly went rigid, his eyes flickering to a spot far to Atlas's left and it wasn't a second later that a third voice broke the silence, "My, my, whatever do we have here."

Atlas looked over to see the man brandishing that bat coated in razor wire, swinging it carelessly as he whistled. Three other men trailed him, each toting their own impressive array of weaponry. The man snarled, "now I hate to break up a lover's quarrel like this, all uninvited and all, but me and my boys were in the neighborhood when we heard you folks being noisy and such out here." He spoke in a grand voice that rattled with every over enunciated syllable like he was a preacher or an old-time judge.

"Now, you wouldn't happen to be the same two lovebirds that disappeared from those women we... how do you say, rehabilitated, would you? The same two that our men saw steal a truck we rightfully earned."

Moose slammed the truck in reverse, motioning to move, but the two side tires were shot almost immediately, flattening in a whirling buzz. "Now, why don't you put that little birdy in park and step out to greet us," the man said. "Mr. and Mr?" He held out a hand in a grand display as if they'd be able to cross the distance to shake it. "Come on now, a little apocalyptic event happens and everyone loses their manners. My name's Dokken, Billy Dokken but my friends over here call me Dokken. Now... I'm gonna give you boys to the count of three to introduce yourselves." He held three fingers straight into the air, dropping one almost immediately. "One."

"Moose!" Moose clambered to answer.

"Moose? Your mom expecting a dog when she had you? Although I can see the resemblance, you big brute." He smiled, a kind of smile that would sear its way across the moon as his pearly teeth shone through stretched lips. "And who might you be with, Moose?"

Atlas didn't speak. Another finger dropped. The man's eyebrows danced. "You really wanna tango, kid?" He half dropped his last finger, letting it quiver for a second, before lazily lowering it to his palm.

The instant it touched, Atlas closed his eyes, shouting, "Atlas! My name... Atlas."

"Atlas and fucking Moose," the man hollered. "What a fucking duo. Did a comic book think you two up? Listen here, kiddos, here's the deal. I'm gonna waddle my beautiful tight ass right over there and check out what goodies you've gathered for us and you're gonna be real still like, would hate to have to have my buddies put a bullet in those pretty lovebird heads of yours."

Atlas's eyes whipped around wildly, motioning as far into his peripherals as he could without moving his head. Nothing but a clearing on either side of them for some twenty feet or so. There was no way they'd make it without being shot down. The men closed the gap between them with ease, Dokken walking straight up and squishing Atlas' face between his fingers, "Ain't you two just the cutest. So fresh, so..." he shook Atlas's jowls, "adorable."

Moose and Atlas stood stiff, both unflinching as Dokken circled his finger through the air, "Boys! Search the truck."

Three men bombarded the truck like crashing boars, ripping whatever contents they could find and spilling them onto the street with no regard to its preservation. Cans of food landed on the ground, rolling under the vehicle. One man grabbed for the jugs of water, unscrewing the lids and spilling them out onto the concrete, all the while chuckling and gallivanting as if performing a playful little sport. Atlas watched their supplies evaporate, everything that was keeping them alive, disappearing in the carnage as the barbarians carelessly wasted the truck's contents.

Dokken reached for a can of beer they had acquired from one of the gas stations, popping open the cap and chugging a bit before tossing the rest aside. He turned towards Atlas and Moose, dropping a can of food on the ground and stomping it open so its contents oozed out onto the pavement. "Oops, silly me, now which one of you's gonna clean that off my boot? How about you, the tall one?" He waggled his shoe where chunks of mystery meat coagulated. Moose didn't flinch. "Maybe you didn't hear me, dog." He waltzed up to Moose, his one hand on the bat, his other moved with the intensity of a freight train, plowing into Moose's ribs so hard he buckled over, and he held Moose down by the hair. "Clean the fucking boot, dog."

Moose dropped to his knees, struggling to breathe, and Atlas stood helplessly as he motioned to pick a chunk off the man's boot. "Nuh-uh-uh," the man cackled, his elongated face breaking out into a wicked grin once more, "Gotta be nice and clean. Use your mouth." He flashed a look at Atlas. "You must be used to sucking filthy meat anyway, eh?"

Moose's eyes raised to meet the man's, murder corrupting his vision as he sputtered for breath. Moose's fist flew faster than Atlas's mind could perceive, flung out wildly, but missed its mark as the man narrowly deflected it. Dokken's foot raised in retaliation, pounding Moose's jaw with so much force that it flung his head backwards. "Now that wasn't very nice, was it?" Dokken walked over, kneeling beside Moose, and whispering, "This is the part where you beg," before twirling around, pacing off a few steps where he shouted, "String them up, boys."

Two men grappled for Moose's limbs, dragging him to his feet as another pair of muscular limbs wrapped Atlas's arms behind his back. "You know, I was gonna let you fuckheads go, out of the kindness of my heart. Show you a little humility for the trouble you caused us, then send you on your way, but no siree. You had to spit all over hospitality." The man circled between them like a vulture, each step causing Atlas to flinch as he prepared for the life ending blow that was sure to come.

Three times he circled his prey, over and over again. And then, just as suddenly, he crashed the bat into Moose's knee, shattering it instantly, yanking on the wires' barbs as they stuck into Moose's skin, tearing off in great globs. Moose screamed, falling backwards, but the men kept him upright. His stitched face broke in two as it clenched around the pain. Atlas dove forward, struggling against those muscular arms with everything he had in him, but it was no use. Dokken revealed a knife holster on his side, dramatically withdrawing a wicked blade and before Atlas could close his eyes, the blade was being thrust into his hand. Atlas was let go. His fingers closed around the cold metallic handle of the blade. He looked around, confused.

Dokken laughed. "Here's the deal, kid. The knife is yours now. You have a decision to make. You swing it at us, maybe kill one of us, and the rest break every bone in both your bodies before leaving you here to rot," he pointed the bat at Moose who quivered before it, "or, you get to live if you gut your boyfriend right now and wear his skin as a fucking coat. Nothing quick, you go for the stomach. I wanna see organs before the light leaves his eyes, understood?"

Atlas tested the blade's weight between his fingers. His body quickly chose its target, and lunged at Dokken, who deflected the blade easily, knocking it free where it clattered to the ground. His fist found Atlas's face, knocking him backward where his head bashed off the truck's door. "Now, you both done fucked yourselves." He reeled his foot back, planting it on Atlas's ribs, who curled up in a desperate attempt to protect his organs from each crashing blow. "I tried being nice. But you reject kindness," his foot slammed Atlas once more, his boot cracking Atlas's ribs. "All that'll be left is malice."

He lunged forward, grappling for Atlas's shoulders and propping him against the side of the car so his head dangled against the driver's seat. Dokken poked Atlas's chest with his bat, gently raising his head with its end so the razor wire brushed his throat. His other hand seized the door, testing its weight, and Atlas realized with horror that he had been lined up just so the door would slam on his head. The razor wire dug deeper into his throat as Dokken added a bit of pressure.

"Keep those eyes on me now, kid. It's no fun if you're not looking me in the eyes. How many slams do you think it'll take to separate your jaw from the skull? To bash in your brain completely? Huh, Moosey, you ever seen Gallagher? Think his head'll explode like a fuckin' watermelon?" He shook his head slightly, his smile perched in the same spot no matter how his head went, "Oh, I've always wanted to try this."

He forced the door open as wide as it would go and Atlas spun, lunging within the truck and curling up on the floor mat. "Stay still and take it like a man, you cock sucking fa-"

In one fluid movement, Atlas reached under the seat, withdrawing the pistol and rolling over onto his back, where he fired off a single shot. The bullet rocketed off his jaw, shattering it instantly. Teeth perforated his throat as Dokken fell to the ground, sputtering incoherent murmurs as his body morphed into a twitching mush.

Atlas stood wobbly to his feet, throwing the pistol at the head of one man before they had a chance to advance on him. They got over their stunned confusion sooner than Atlas was hoping, advancing on him, their weapons drawn. Atlas quivered, struggling to keep his footing as the first reached him, swinging a machete at Atlas. He dodged, weaved, and knocked the man aside, taking on the second. The man charged but was immediately trumpeted off his feet as a thunderous roar ripped through the air while a bullet launched through his chest. Atlas and the last two men turned. Moose had crawled over to Dokken's body and unholstered his gun, which now wavered through the air, flipping between the two men. Another shot blasted the one as the other lunged for Atlas, wrapping his arm around him and using him as a shield. A pistol grazed Atlas's temple right above his ear.

"Drop it or your boyfriend gets his brains blown out," the man squealed from somewhere behind Atlas. Moose dropped the gun to the ground. The man's pistol snapped off Atlas's head, pointed directly at Moose, but before he could pull the trigger, Atlas lurched around, snapping his teeth into the man's neck. He tore, with all his might, a chunk from the man's throat. The pistol went off, the bullet ricocheting off the pavement a few feet from Moose's head.

Both Atlas and the man fell backwards, slamming the truck's side where they slowly slid down to the ground. Atlas kept biting, ripping into the man's throat in a blind hunger. The man screamed, his throat muscles vibrating within Atlas's mouth, gushing with pools of blood as he shredded the dying body. His teeth clunked against the bone. His mouth went numb as more and more pounds of flesh were stuffed between his cheeks.

He kept eating until well after the screaming had ended, not stopping until the sputtering muscles halted their twitching within his mouth. As the body ran heat down his pulsating throat. A hand reached out for him, tugging his shoulder and his teeth snapped out at it, catching only the air as Moose withdrew faster than he could. He looked into Moose's eyes, and he thought about killing him. He contemplated it. Tearing into Moose's skull or bashing it against the ground until a viscous fluid poured out his eyes. His body tensed, ready for the kill shot as his eyes shot to vital points on Moose's body.

Atlas sighed, breathing in and out deliberately as he closed his eyes, attempting to calm that pounding fury in his chest. He heard Moose's voice, but couldn't make out what he was saying over the demanding drums of his own heartbeat. He held his breath for as long as he could, only breathing out again when the desperate beast inside him had calmed enough that he could look at Moose and truly see him. Moose's face was distorted, like he was hiding the disgust Atlas knew he must be feeling. He was acutely aware of the blood that painted his body like a canvas, coming in violent streaks, sticking to the folds of his skin. "Don't look at me. Not with those eyes. Not right now."

Moose's eyes dropped. A killer. He had been so afraid of becoming a killer now he had to watch Atlas mercilessly devour a man. Still, when Moose's eyes returned to him, they were filled with an outer casing of love, biting through the fear and anguish.

Moose held out a hand once more, tentative, his body ready to pull it back at any second. "Come on, we have to leave before more of them show up."

Atlas took his hand. His body fluttered with fear as his instincts fought to yank Moose in and instead let Moose help him to his feet. "The... the truck. How are we supposed to?"

"They came from that way. I assume they have a vehicle of some sort not far from here. You're gonna have to drive, though. Fucker destroyed my leg. Do you think you're capable?"

"I... I have to be. We have to get you to that safe zone. We're so close."

"Not even a day's drive. Maybe four more hours and we'll be there."

Chapter Twelve

ATLAS DROVE THE JEEP they had found, his mind blinking in and out of existence as he fought for consciousness. His eyes flicked to his reflection in the mirror, shirtless and coated in blood and little chunks of flesh like daisy dot freckles on his skin. He could feel the blood coagulating in the sun, heating his chest and neck as they drove. Atlas's head swam as the infection ate away at his brain. He looked over at Moose through the dots that danced over his vision. Moose had noticeably paled, nursing his cracked leg as he leaned back in the seat, his breathing coming in sporadic intervals and laying heavy like each breath had to snake its way through miles to escape.

The radio played that song, over and over, coming in clearer than ever as Cat Voleur's voice stretched through the open air. Atlas drove despite the disconnection he felt from his own body, his limbs acting on their own accord to get them to their final destination. He viewed his limbs with such a strong detachment it was like he was playing a game, piloting some weird mech suit that looked like him as his spirit nearly left his body. He faded in and out for what could've been hours, desperate to keep the truck moving until his foot drug off the gas, relinquishing the movement of the car as it lazed to a halt.

"What are you stopping for?"

"Get out."

"What?"

"This is as far as I go."

Moose looked over at him, as he couldn't help his eyes from frothing over with tears. "Don't make this any harder than it needs to be. We both knew it was gonna come to this." Moose went to push in closer to Atlas, who peeled back against the wall, gripping his temple with his fingers as his very skull itself burned. "Don't- don't come close. Please, I- I can't, just don't come any closer."

His eyes latched around an empty spot, not daring to look straight at Moose as he hovered in Atlas's peripherals. Atlas reached around the back seat, digging his hand into his backpack. He shoved his manuscript into Moose's hand without moving his eyes once. "Besides, you're gonna have the most important part of me with you, this part of me. This is how I live on, through this, and through you."

Moose stared down at his hands, silently studying the details that ran through his palms. "Moose, talk to me. What are you thinking? Moose?"

"You know you could bite me. Infect me. We could be together."

"You still don't get it, do you? Once I start... I can't stop. It's like the worst addiction I've ever had, each hit only satisfying enough to get to the next. You're still pure, you're still-"

"Atlas-"

"You're not built for this... this... whatever it is, Moose. This isn't life. I've already died, Moose, from the second that blood entered my body, I was dead. I'm a husk. You don't want this. What? Why are you staring at me like that?"

Moose gulped, eyes peering somewhere to Atlas' side, "We could kill ourselves, we could... we could just go out together. Just the two of us, just now. Atlas, we can do this together. We don't have to be separated... we don't have to be alone."

Atlas glared at him, watching him squirm under his own thoughts. "You won't be alone... Moose. You won't be... I won't be."

"I love you, Atlas. You don't have to say it back," he stared down the manuscript thoughtfully, "you never did. You had to be there. I just want you to be there."

"Moose-"

"I know, I know. I need to leave. This needs to happen. It's hard. I don't know how to do this. I'm scared and I don't know how, and I feel so alone and-" Moose rambled on, barely breaking to breathe.

"Moose..." Atlas sighed, his eyes finally meeting Moose's and for a split second he lost even his aggressive hunger in those eyes. Those beautiful, piercing eyes. "Moose, I love you. I'm sorry I didn't say it sooner, but I always have. Ever since we met, before your name ever touched my tongue, before it even existed in my universe, I have loved you every single day of my existence. But now- now all I can think about is killing you. It's festering within me. Even now, even in these few moments I'm speaking, it's all that invades my mind. I'm a cancer, just that, only that. Moose, I've loved you, and I will love you, until my very last thought. I'll taste your name on my dying breath, but that's all I'll be at this point, dying. So, you need to leave now..."

"I can't. I can't live without you. I'm sorry, Atlas. I can't."

"You have to. You don't get a choice, just like I don't get one now. This is just something you have to do."

Moose shot out a hand, gently running it across the outline of Atlas's jawline as he squirmed against the drive to snap completely. He could feel the blood smudging on his skin as Moose's fingers ice skated over it, coming to a stop at his chin and slowly angling him so he had to look square at Moose. Moose leaned in close, their lips brushed, Moose's hot breath causing the little hairs on Atlas's face to sway. Atlas's toes curled in anticipation as their lips connected, one final, heart racing kiss as they latched onto each other. For a second, Atlas's fears melted away and then he was lightly pushing Moose away from him, disconnecting from him and allowing his gaze to drop once more.

Moose stared silently for a moment, pushing open the door and quietly abandoning the car, carrying only the manuscript, the backpack jangling as he walked. Atlas watched his lover limp off into the woods, and quickly as he disappeared, he felt the sickness take him over completely, finally able to surrender himself to temptation as his mind melted into the background, only existing in the subtle glimpse of lingering thoughts. He noticed his reflection in the mirror, but those eyes were no longer his own, two blank coins staring from his skull like a taxidermized version of himself. He slammed his hands against the steering wheel, feeling his wrists crack with the force, anything to ground himself, but it was no use.

Tears streamed down his face as his body moved on its own accord, diving out of the jeep in odd jangly movements that tore at the muscles without really caring. His injuries didn't hold him back anymore. The pain was still present, but the instinct to prevent it had melted away completely. His nose sniffed the air, immediately picking up Moose's scent, and his stomach dropped as his body shambled forward, tracking the man he had let go.

His body jerked through the woods, and his fears were confirmed as he came to a clearing where he saw Moose limping in the distance. Moose spun around, his face lifting for a second before dropping in his confusion, shifting to fear in an instant as Atlas's body fought to close the space between them. Atlas forced open his jaw, squealing out the few words he could. "Run! Please, run!"

Moose turned, picking up speed, but his crippled leg was holding him back. He was no match for Atlas's blind intuition. Atlas watched helplessly. He was no longer piloting his body. The foreign invader that controlled his actions barreled towards Moose with a hunger no longer held back by human emotions. Atlas watched. He could only watch, hope for Moose's safety waning as the space between them grew smaller and smaller.

In an instant, Atlas was on top of him, tackling Moose to the ground, where he bit down on anything he could. He felt his teeth catch something, tearing chunks out of it. Not flesh. Atlas was flooded with relief. Not flesh. Only the backpack. Still, his mouth swiveled, desperate to get around it as Moose struggled helplessly against him. He was almost on Moose's throat when a snapping branch drew both of their eyes.

A single woman stood in front of them, a pistol drawn. Atlas stood, thank God he stood, leaving Moose laying in the dirt as he tentatively approached the new figure. A nametag bounced off her chest, "Cat Voleur". They had made it. Moose was safe. Still, Atlas couldn't stop his body from advancing on the woman. Her eyes locked on Moose. "Have you been bitten?" She commanded. No response. "Have you?"

Atlas held his breath, his body slowing slightly as if still in a slur of his control, until Moose finally answered, "No. No, I'm fine."

Atlas's body let go, charging down the woman and watched as her pistol went off, smoke erupting from the barrel, and he closed his eyes, finally accepting the death that followed.

About the Author

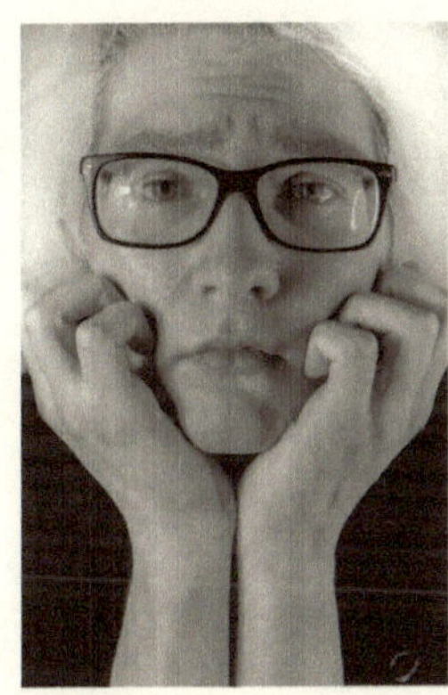

I'm just a weirdo who constantly measures mantras between 'in omnia paratus' and 'memento mori.' I love puzzle work poems and songs that require research to decipher the full meaning of turning poems into games of their own meaning, as well as horror that digs deep into the crevices of the mind to pull away layers of deep-seated fear. I'm the author of CALL TO THE VOID DEFINITIVE EDITION and THE EMPTY SPACE BETWEEN THE STARS, two short story collections. I am excited to share my first novella with you!

I want to extend a sincere thank you to everyone that picked up my first novella, SLEEPING AMONG WOLVES. I appreciate anyone that takes time out of their lives to indulge in my creations. The characters of Atlas and Moose blossomed into their own in a way I had never anticipated, quickly becoming my favorite characters I've written to date. The story is an expression of my own fears, masked by young love and defiance in a reflection of our world today.

Fear and romance have always gone hand in hand for me, my two favorite genres to create, and this is my first time mashing up the two into their own bittersweet universe. SLEEPING AMONG WOLVES means a lot of things to me, and will hopefully strike a chord with you, and I wish you luck in finding your own meaning to take from it. Again, thank you!